To Cheryl,
because you are.

Into the face of the devil

A love story from the California gold rush
(A Tom Marsh adventure, book 2)
By John Rose Putnam

"Courage is resistance to fear,
mastery of fear,
not absence of fear."
Mark Twain

Copyright © Statement

Published by John Rose Putnam
ISBN 978-0-9909629-1-5

1

I heard a pistol pop and the tinkle of glass shattering. It was hardly noon and the fresh-off-the-boat guys were at it again. While I pulled my freight wagon over at the new hotel down the street more drunks fired off shots. Hot lead splattered across my load of lumber scaring me half out of my boots. I leaped to the ground and ducked behind a stack of planks, shaking like a leaf. Then a fierce clatter of pounding hooves came from up the road and the city boys grabbed their hats and ran for their lives. A buckboard raced toward me like the hounds of hell were after it.

"Hiyah! Get on now," my friend Eban hollered, snapping the reins so the horses would run even faster while Woody Dunn, a muleskinner a little older than me, held onto the seat next to him, a frightful look smeared across his mug. I stood up and waved. Woody caught sight of me and jumped to the ground, somehow managing to stay on his feet when he hit.

"What's wrong, Woody?" I asked. "Where's Eban heading in such a rush?"

Woody sucked up fresh air like he hadn't had any in a month. "Tom, you got to get to the cafe quick," he wheezed. "Maggie needs you to look after the place for her. She ain't doing good and Joshua took her up to the cabin."

"Maggie!" I blurted. "Is it time?" I could see the uneasiness deep in his eyes.

"She's asking for Mrs. Wimmer and Eban's heading over to Coloma right now to fetch her," he said. "But don't you dare go near the cabin. That's women's stuff. Leave it alone. You'd best take care of the cafe like Maggie wants."

My feet went cold as a February snow. Even though I'd promised Maggie I'd tend to things for her the whole idea of me cooking for a bunch of cantankerous miners scared me silly. "Woody, most of those men don't only eat at the cafe for the food, they come to see Maggie. She's about the only woman around and for sure the best cook. They'll be ornery as starving wolves if I'm there instead of her."

Woody nodded his head and laughed. "Yep, like as not there'll be some awful sore gold miners, but they'll get used to it. Besides somebody's got to do it and you're the one Maggie wants. I'll unload your wagon. You head to the cafe."

When I stood there like a one legged man at a barn dance Woody gave me a shove on the shoulder. "Go on, Tom," he said, still grinning at my complete discombobulation.

I started toward the cafe on foot, but in the short spell while I'd talked to Woody the mob of fresh-off-the-boat guys had filled the street once more. Mostly from New York City or some other place back east, they didn't know the first thing about mining gold. Folks who'd been in California a while looked down their noses at them, figuring they were nothing but trouble.

The old timers were right. For the last couple of days they'd caused a heck of a hullabaloo here in the middle of town drinking, yelling and showing off their new colt revolvers. And now I worried they would start shooting again so I glanced back toward the pile of boards where I hid earlier.

A fellow I couldn't see yelled out from over by the saloon, "Quiet down and listen up." Right off the shouting and shoving eased. "That's better," he went on.

That made me feel some safer too. And while I scouted around for an easy way through the crowd, the guy started talking in a high, twangy voice.

"I know you're worried about all the robberies and killings happening lately," he told them. "It's a bad thing, but I'm here to help. It's getting harder for a man to find a good paying strike as more men show up in the mines. Folks can get desperate and do some rotten things, but you ain't got to worry if you're a part of the California Mining Cooperative. We got solid, gold producing claims, some in the best dry diggings you'll find anywhere and others right on the creek. You can make money tomorrow, no prospecting place after place looking for color. All you do is sign up. I'll even buy you a drink. Come on inside. Let's talk it over. Who's first?"

A loud cheer went up and the men pushed past me toward the flap of the big tent everybody called the Round Tent Saloon. In no time I had the street to myself. I hustled toward the cafe and reflected on how fast things had changed here in Hangtown. This time last year, when Maggie, Joshua and Eban first came, there were no buildings at all. Now the freight line hauled in lumber from the saw mill at Coloma for each new store built. Plus we made regular trips to Sacramento City for food, supplies and all the other stuff folks needed to live.

Maggie's Cafe did a booming business, too. What with all these men here digging gold and almost no women at all, it was the one place a man could go to get anything like a home cooked meal. And it didn't much matter if a fellow had been in Hangtown for a while or if he just got off the boat, they all needed to eat and most of them could barely make coffee. Maggie was the most popular person in town and I was as proud to be her friend as I could be.

Right before I got to the cafe I looked past the log bridge that crossed Hangtown Creek and up to the cabin perched on the hill. Maggie was there now, in the bedroom she shared with Joshua behind the dormer window on the left side of the attic. Eban had the bedroom on the right and I slept in a little room downstairs behind the kitchen. She took me in last fall after Pa and my two brothers died. Alone and near starved to death in Coloma, I'd loaded wagons at the saw mill for whatever I could get. I owed her an awful lot. She'd become a second mother and a big sister all rolled into one. I would run the cafe if she wanted. I'd do anything for Maggie.

The little bell that hung on the front door jingled when I walked inside. I crossed the empty dining room and closed the shutters on a four-foot opening over a counter in the center of the south wall where Maggie passed out plates of food when she worked by herself. I didn't want anybody gawking at me while I cooked. Then I went through the door to the kitchen.

In the middle of the east wall a venison stew warmed on the stove. Bowls of cut up potatoes, carrots and onions and a black iron pot that held a big hunk of beef sat on the table in front. It looked like Maggie had been fixing a pot roast right before she'd gone. I rolled up my sleeves, tossed the blue army cap Joshua had given me on a chair and started in where she left off. It had to be done—even though I dreaded what the miner's would say when they discovered Maggie wasn't here.

Even with both windows open wide no hint of a mid-afternoon breeze blew into the café's kitchen. Standing over a tin tub of hot wash water my own sweat soaked through my gray wool shirt and seeped under the blue bandana wrapped around my head. I'd been miserable enough when I first got here but I felt even worse now.

Maybe things wouldn't be so bad if the miners didn't act so downright disagreeable when they found Maggie laid up and that I'd fixed everything they ate today. One dandy in a flashy silk vest, fresh off the boat from back east somewhere, had stormed out yelling that unrendered hog fat tasted better than my buttermilk biscuits. Another guy from New Orleans cussed me out in French for what seemed like forever. At least I think he was cussing, I didn't understand a word he said. And after that a red-haired sailor from some place called Australia told me that the stuff his dog threw up when he was sick looked more appealing than my pot roast.

I sure didn't feel up for this, but I knew I had to do it. Maggie depended on me. Back on our farm I'd done most of the cooking and my Pa and brothers liked it fine. But Maggie's scrumptious food had folks who ate here spoiled rotten. I supposed they'd get over it and I tried not to worry about it much. Still, I'd be awful grateful when I could get back to driving a team of slow, stubborn mules again. But with Maggie's condition nobody could say when that would be.

The bell on the door rang out and I rolled my eyes toward the ceiling, dropped the plate I'd washed back into the water and dried my hands on my pants. Likely more miners had come for an early supper, and they would probably yell at me about the food too. I ripped off the bandana, mopped my hair with a towel and strode to the door, my head high, my jaw forward. If anybody didn't like my cooking they could go back to their shanty and have the same salt pork and beans miners usually eat.

Inside the dining room I saw the front door open wide. Two men who'd been sitting at a table close by the window waited outside on Morton, a crotchety old cuss who still had on the same filthy wool shirt and pants he did a month ago. He hadn't finished his meal yet but when he saw me coming he pushed his plate back and stood. "It ain't right you charge the same when Maggie ain't working." he grumbled. "You ain't near the cook she is."

Who cares, I thought. I wanted to yell at him but instead took a deep breath and remembered my manners. "She'll be back soon, Mr. Morton. She'd love to see you then," I said as nice as I could.

Morton wagged a grubby finger in my face. "Ain't eating

here again 'less she's cooking. You hear me?" he groused.

I had a sudden notion to throw a plate at his head, but somehow muzzled the urge. "Suit yourself, sir," I said with a snap to my words.

Morton muttered something under his breath, turned and walked outside to join his partners, leaving the door open. When I bent over the table to scrape and stack the plates the last two customers got up to leave. I didn't know either of them off hand, but they had on clothes way too fancy for miners. Maybe they were new in town, so many men were, but they didn't look like any of the fresh-off-the-boat guys that had flooded into the gold country lately either.

The skinnier one glanced over to me. "Are you running this place by yourself, son?" he asked in a thin, twangy voice that sounded like the guy at the Round Tent earlier. He had on a well-made black suit and fancy handmade Mexican riding boots. But his big ears and long, clean-shaved jaw reminded me of the triangle I'd learned about in my arithmetic primer. The other guy, beefier with a bushy moustache under a wide, fat nose way too big for his pudgy face, wore a plain blue work shirt and black wool pants but had on a pair of fancy Mexican boots too.

I squeezed up my best smile. It couldn't hurt. "Only for a few days, sir. I hope."

The man threw some coins on the table and followed his companion toward the door. I grabbed my stack of dishes and turned to the kitchen when he stopped in front of me, blocking my way. I gulped. Here it comes, I thought.

"Son, the fellow you just talked with complained the whole time about the food. Well, you might want to know that my friend and I enjoyed our meal quite a bit," he said with a touch of a smile tarnished by a missing front tooth.

"Thank you, sir," I replied, all at once feeling a whole lot better. "I'm glad somebody liked my cooking. Folks been giving me the dickens about it since Maggie left, but she'll be back soon." It was the first nice thing anybody said to me all day. It did me a world of good.

After a quick peek toward his friend, the man added, "Well, I wish her the best. I'll make it a point to eat here again when she's back. Good day to you."

"She'll be glad to see you, sir." I said.

He tossed on a flat-topped hat and strode to the open door, but right when he did somebody else showed up, somebody in a dress. He quickly stopped and doffed his black hat. "Good afternoon, miss. I must say you look lovely today," he crooned. His voice sounded sweet and slick all of a sudden, like a quart of molasses got dumped into it.

"Lovely! Bah!" the girl moaned. "I'm tired, hot and hungry. And you, sir, are in my way." The man eased to his left but just as she marched by him she stopped dead in her tracks. "Oh! You lecher!" she shrieked and swung a blue-checked gingham handbag right at his head. He ducked it easy and slipped off, chuckling to himself.

The bell clanged loud when she slammed the door. Holy Moses, I thought, she's as mad as all get out and she's in here. I dropped the dishes back on the table.

She'd stopped just inside the room, and as I looked up at her my eyes near popped from my face. A field of blue flowers on a yellow calico dress shrank to a pencil-thin waist only to billow out wide again before it stopped at a slender, lace-edged collar. A pretty turned-up nose over pouting red lips separated her fiery blue eyes, while a lock of yellow hair dangled temptingly below each ear and left me longing to see what else she had tucked away underneath her blue and white bonnet. And with the sweet, flowery scent that came in when she did tossed on top of how she looked I couldn't drag my eyes away from her.

I hadn't known many girls my age. There were two buck toothed tomboys on a farm three miles from where I grew up and I did meet a few who were with the wagon trains that stopped at Diamond Springs last fall, but none of them struck me as anywhere near as fetching as this one. Women in the gold country were as rare as hen's teeth but girls—there just weren't any.

"Well, are you going to show me to a seat or not?" she demanded.

That snapped me back from my woolgathering. Her voice had changed. The anger stayed but a whiney, pouting tone fluttered on top. Maybe something was wrong with her? There were ten tables, each with four chairs, so why should I have to show her a place to sit? Then I remembered a story I'd read in McGuffey's Reader. It happened back east somewhere and the men always helped women into chairs and stuff. She must be an eastern girl and didn't know how we did things here in the gold mines.

Still, I didn't have to squeeze up a smile now. I beamed. "Would you like a place by the window?" I asked. She nodded and broke into a bright grin. A thrill rushed right through my gut. My knees got wobbly and my heart thumped like a runaway stallion, but somehow I managed to get her settled into the chair.

She batted her lashes again and the stallion raced even faster. "The old man who drove the wagon said I should come in here and somebody named Tom would see I got something to eat. Do you know where I can find Tom?" she asked real sweet.

"The old man?" My heart reined back to a walk. "Do you mean Eban?" The thrill in my gut twisted into a knot. This girl wasn't from back east, at least not lately. She'd come from Coloma with Eban. She was in trouble, just like I'd been when Eban found me there, loading wagons at the saw mill and slowly starving. Eban wouldn't have brought her here otherwise.

She flashed her pearly white teeth at me again. "Yes, that's his name, Eban," she cooed.

"Well, I'm Tom, Tom Marsh. I'll get you some pot roast and a glass of well water. Would that be okay?"

"Oh yes! I'm so hungry." For the first time I noticed the fear that lurked in the corners of her eyes. I knew that fear all too well, and the hunger that went with it. I would feed her. We could talk later.

"Don't worry. You're safe here." I promised.

Tears misted over the fear, but somehow she kept her smile. "Eban said I would like you. I think I do. I'm Lacey, Lacey Lawson."

"Pleased to meet you, Lacey. You wait here. I won't be long." I couldn't help but grin at her. I grabbed the stack of plates, ducked into the kitchen and quickly hustled back with another dish brimming with pot roast, biscuits, and potatoes and carrots on the side, plus a pitcher of cool well water and a hot cup of coffee. Lacey's eyes bulged wide as her gaze followed me across the room. When I put the plate down in front of her she dived into the food like a hawk onto a ground squirrel, mumbling something that sounded like a thank you.

"I'll be in the back. If you need something, anything at all, just holler," I said and she glanced up, chewing wildly, and nodded. Lacey Lawson was a real pretty girl who happened to be awful hungry right now.

I went back to the kitchen and started in on the pile of dirty dishes that waited, but my mind stuck on Lacey. Almost every day I drove a wagon over the hill to Coloma and there weren't many women there either. Coloma had grown like mushrooms do after a spring rain, but it had stayed a rough and tumble gold town. A girl like Lacey didn't belong there anymore than she belonged here.

I'll never forget how I got to Coloma about this time last summer with Pa and my brothers. Right off two vicious desperados murdered Hank and Jess. After that Pa gave up. He didn't last much longer. My whole life fell apart. I had to struggle hard just to scrape enough food together to stay alive. The memory of the empty, gnawing hunger that ate at my gut from sunup till dark, day in and day out, will always be with me.

Then Eban showed up and gave me a job with the freight company. My world changed overnight. He brought me here and introduced me to Maggie and Joshua. It was a second chance in life. In no time they were like my brand new family. And I sure am grateful for all they've done for me.

Today Maggie had pains and everybody said that meant her baby was coming so Eban rushed off to Coloma to get Mrs. Wimmer. She probably knew more about birthing babies than anyone else here in the foothills, with most of that learning real personal. She had a huge family, totally out of place in a town full of almost nobody but miners. But she had a right. Her husband ran the saw mill where they first found gold. She was there before any of the prospectors.

Mrs. Wimmer also had a big heart and I knew that once she noticed Lacey she would've corralled her just like she did me that day when poor Jess washed up by the millrace dam with his throat slashed. First she dragged me to her cabin and fed me breakfast. Later she took me to the burial service. And when Pa showed up so drunk he couldn't stand she gave a bone chilling prophesy about what life would be like for a fifteen-year old boy alone in a gold rush boomtown. Everything she said came true. The same things would be in store for a girl like Lacey, only worse.

I pulled the dishes from the rinse water and gave them a quick dry. The bell on the front door hadn't jingled in a while so I figured 1 had enough time before the supper rush to whip up some peach cobbler. I'd never baked a pie before but Maggie wrote down how she did it. She said a cobbler would be the easiest to make because I wouldn't have to worry about a crust.

I mixed up the flour and stuff in a bowl, poured the peaches into buttered pie pans and dabbed the batter into the peaches with a spoon. It all seemed pretty easy and it looked like it did when Maggie made it so I pitched two logs into the firebox and slid the pie pans into the oven, already hoping some would be left over to have after my own supper. After all, peach cobbler was my favorite.

While I wiped down the table with an old rag, I got an uneasy feeling like somebody watched me. I wheeled toward the dining room door. Lacey stood there smiling, the blue-checked bonnet gone and her blonde hair piled up in a neat bun.

She leaned back against the doorjamb and twirled one of the curls that hung in front of her ear around her finger. "Say, you're real handy in the kitchen for a boy. How'd you learn to make cobbler anyway?" she asked, sassy like.

Right off that sounded pretty snotty to me. "What are you doing here?" I barked back.

My growl didn't seem to bother her much. "I'm looking for my Papa, if it's any of your business," she answered and rolled her eyes to the ceiling.

"This ain't no place for a girl like you," I added, still miffed at her.

She pushed her arm out straight and gazed down a slender finger pointed right at my feet. "Did you know your britches are too short?" she asked.

I looked right down at my boots and felt my face flush. I'd gotten the hand-me-down pants from Jess and like most of my clothes they'd grown old and ragged. Nobody else in town seemed to mind, yet for some reason it bothered me a lot that she did. "I planned to get another pair soon." I stammered. "Maggie says I've grown a bunch this last year." Maggie was right. I measured close to six feet now and it didn't look like I would stop growing anytime soon.

She put a hand to her mouth to muzzle a laugh. "I'm sorry. Papa says I have a mean streak in me. I think you're a right handsome young man—the best I've seen in a while. But your britches are still too short," and a tiny giggle slipped between her fingers.

All at once I realized I wasn't mad at Lacey anymore, but she did stupefy me. I really wanted her to like me and when she'd called me handsome my heart thundered again. Then she went right back to the pants thing and I fell flat in a puddle. I didn't know what to think, or do, or say. "I, uh, I—"

"In San Francisco men can get ready-made britches that fit. You buy the ones that go around your waist and then roll up the legs. It's all the rage, you know." Her tone felt softer now and sounded more like she cared.

I'd seen a lot of new miners who came to town lately wearing rolled up pants, but I hadn't thought much about them. And for some reason it seemed like my pants were more important to Lacey than they were to me. "I don't get to San Francisco much. I reckon I'll just have to make do," I said, thinking that ought to end the whole thing.

But Lacey pushed past me and walked to the back door. She grabbed one of Maggie's aprons from a peg and held it up in front of her. It had blue and white checks like her bonnet and looked real good against the yellow dress. Still, it was Maggie's apron and I wasn't sure what Lacey planned on doing with it. "That's Maggie's, you know," I said as gentle as I could.

"Do you think she would mind if I helped you out a little?" Lacey said as she slid the apron on and tied it behind her.

I stared at her wide-eyed. "Help me . . .?" I stammered, wondering how in the world she'd already become the most confounding creature I'd ever known when the bell on the front door cut short my pondering.

Before I could gather what remained of my senses she sashayed right past me, the blue flowers on her round bottom swaying easily back and forth. At the door she stopped and turned to me. "Yeah, I'll help you. Watch this." She winked and disappeared.

I followed her but before I got out of the kitchen I heard her say, "Hi there, gentlemen. My name's Lacey and I'll be helping Maggie here for a while. How are you?" Sweetness and honey practically dripped from her voice.

"Glad to meet you, Lacey. I'm Jed."

"Don't pay no attention to my little brother, Lacey. My name's Jeremiah and I'd be pleased to walk you home after you're done here."

"Oh, aren't you special, both of you," she gushed. "We're having a wonderful pot roast today and peach cobbler for dessert.

How about I bring you some hot coffee for starters?"

I got to the dining room in time to see her spin from the table and sashay towards me again like she'd just done in the kitchen. But this time the eyes of the two Wiggins boys had stuck on the pretty blue flowers that swished to and fro with each step she took. Jeremiah Wiggins was so roped in by her that he'd turned all the way around in his chair to watch, and leaned against the back so hard I thought he'd topple flat on his face.

Lacey winked again then swung by me into the kitchen. My insides, already in a muddle, flopped around like a fish out of water. The Wiggins boys were about my age but Jeremiah was part of the rowdy crowd in town. I didn't care much for them anyway, and now that they flirted with Lacey I'd gotten downright steamed—until she'd winked at me. Then everything seemed funny, like she was trifling with them—or was she trifling with me? Oh, Lord, I thought, what's happening?

Before I could clear my head she blew by me again, a coffee pot and two cups in her hands. As she plunked the cups on the table and filled them, I decided that I'd seen enough and went back to the kitchen to check on the cobbler and maybe whip up some more biscuits.

##

The bell on the front door dinged for what seemed like the nine-hundredth time, but chances were it would be the last tonight. I mopped the sweat from my forehead, picked up two small plates from the table and headed to the dining room. Once inside I could see Lacey in the lamplight, talking to someone standing in the dark outside the door.

"Now don't you worry. I'll be working here for a while. Why don't you come back tomorrow?" she said but sometime during the long afternoon she'd lost her honey-flavored tone. Now she sounded plain tired.

"Well, yes'm. That pot roast was sure the best I ever had, and I'll be back, you bet. But I'd hate to have anything happen to you on your way home. This is a rough town, you know, and if I was walking with you you'd be a lot safer," the voice from outside pled.

"Now aren't you sweet, but I'll be just fine. I'll see you tomorrow then." The bell rang loud as she slammed the door harder than necessary. She turned, leaned back against it and slid slowly to the floor, letting out a long, pitiful moan as she did.

She sat with her legs spread wide and her hands on the floor. Her head hung low against her chest while sweat streaked across her forehead then dripped from her nose. Her blonde hair, once so neat, dangled willy-nilly out of the bun. I already knew the back of her yellow dress had been soaked through with sweat for hours. I couldn't tell about the front because of Maggie's apron. And, in spite of it all, right now Lacey Lawson was the prettiest girl in the whole world.

I walked up to her, squatted on my haunches, and held out one of the plates. "Peach cobbler? It's the last of it."

Her tired eyes rolled up, followed by her head. With a grunt she raised her left hand to take the plate. With her right she patted the floor. I accepted and scooted up against the doorjamb next to her.

She slouched into my shoulder and held up the pie. "Do you always have dessert before supper?"

"No, this is the first time." I said and realized that my voice carried all the same signs of a long day of hard work in the heat as hers did.

"Good idea," she said and took a big bite of the cobbler.

"Yeah," I agreed and we each ate our pie without talking. I finished first and dropped my plate on the floor. "How long were you at Mrs. Wimmer's?" I asked.

"What makes you think I was at Mrs. Wimmer's?" she retorted and put her empty plate down beside mine.

"Just a guess, but then I wonder why you were so hungry if you were with her."

She pulled her knees up to her chest and wrapped her arms around them. "Well, you're kind of right, but not completely. I just got to Coloma when Mrs. Wimmer ran into me. I think the man who brought me up from Sacramento City sent word to her. She took me home and that's when the old man—what's his name again?"

"Eban."

"Yeah, that's when Eban showed up and off we went lickety-split. She had promised to feed me but babies are more important, I guess."

"Did Eban ask you to help out here in the cafe?" I reached out, picked up her plate and piled it on top of mine.

"For a guy whose britches are too short you're pretty smart.

Did you guess that too?" she asked but now she sounded way too tired to seem sassy or snotty.

"Eban found me in Coloma a while back, too. He gave me a job with the freight line. That job saved my life."

"Are you telling me that working in this cafe is going to save my life, Mr. Short Britches?" Now I heard a touch of sass sneak back into her tone.

I ignored it, too tired to fight. "Well, I don't know, but just like that last customer said, this is a gold town and it's a rough place, especially for a girl."

"How about this Maggie, she's doing okay here isn't she? Why can't I?"

"Maggie's had more than her fair share of hard times, way more than her share."

Lacey leaned over and caught my eye. "You like Maggie a lot don't you? Like maybe even more than peach cobbler?" she said softly, even managing a tired smile.

I had to laugh. She sure had a way about her. "Yeah, I like her way more than peach cobbler. That's a fact. I think you'll like her too when you get to meet her. Maggie's pretty darn special." I stood up with the pie plates in my left hand and offered her my right. "How about we finish up that pot roast? You still hungry?" I asked.

She grinned, a worn, sore grin but an honest one. "You bet I am. I could eat the whole cow, hooves and all." She let me pull her to her feet and took my arm. Together we walked into the kitchen where we piled as much food onto our plates as we possibly could before we went back into the dining room and sat at a table by an open window.

After I'd eaten most of my supper I finally felt full enough to talk again. "You did a really great job today. I'm pretty sure we had way more business than Maggie usually does on a Friday. The word must've got out that you were here and the miners turned out in droves. By tomorrow everybody for twenty miles around will know your name. With Maggie laid up having the baby and all you'll be the only girl around. Every lonely miner in town will come to see you. We're liable to be swamped."

Lacey kept her head down, picking at her carrots, but it seemed to me that her face had gone from plain white to a deep red. Then again, it could just be the lamps. "Oh, I don't know," she mumbled. "Maybe it was your cooking. The pot roast really was great and the cobbler was wonderful."

"Yeah, well, everybody thought my cooking was rotten until you showed up. Then all of a sudden it got good. Does food taste better just because a pretty girl gives it to you?"

She giggled, her head still down, her face still red. "Maybe it does at that."

"This country is full of men who left their wives and families to come here to mine. There are a lot more who should have been looking for a wife to start a family with but instead they came here. Right now you're probably the only unmarried female east of Sacramento City, and if you aren't I'd bet a Yankee dollar to a horseshoe nail that you're the prettiest. Tomorrow's Saturday, we'll be busier than a beehive in clover."

"Oh Lord," she whispered but I barely heard what she said. Her voice suddenly went soft and squeaky and her face didn't seem so dark any more. In fact it seemed as white as a clean bed sheet now. In a flash of panic I thought maybe my pot roast had made her sick.

"You're looking pale. Are you feeling okay?" I quizzed.

She hunkered lower in her chair. "Oh, it must be the light in here."

I turned to see if the lamps had run out of oil or something, but both burned bright and strong.

From outside came the clomp stomp of two quick footsteps. The door pushed open, the bell jangled, a boot stepped in from the dark. "We're closed, mister," I blurted.

Before the words made it all the way out I realized my mistake, but Eban grinned wide behind his gray beard as he closed the door and threw the latch.

"I hear you've been busy," he said and tossed his straw hat on a table.

I muttered something close to a yes while Lacey rolled her eyes.

Eban took it in stride. "Three people stopped me on the way here from the cabin. They all praised the food, complimented Lacey and commented on how crowded the cafe seemed. And looking at you two I'd say you earned your pay today." He turned a chair around backwards and sat down, folding his arms on top of the backrest.

I looked across at Lacey. She stared at me from red, weary

eyes. "Lacey did great, Eban. Everybody loved her."

"No!" She perked up and grabbed Eban's arm to make her point. "Tom's cooking is wonderful. All the men said so." She turned back to me. "How'd you learn to cook like that, anyway?" She sounded like she really meant it, but somehow I thought I saw a glint of the fear I'd noticed this afternoon lurking in her eyes again.

Eban spread his hands wide, palms up and looked from Lacey to me. "Now you two hang on a minute," he said. "I came to tell you that Maggie had her baby, and both mama and little Josie Tomasina Stone are doing great. Tom, you're a godfather."

"Me, a godfather? Holy Moses!" The words gushed out of my mouth. I didn't know what else to say, and besides Lacey suddenly beamed at me like I'd done something important, and that made me feel kind of fluttery deep down, like a covey of quail got loose in my innards.

Eban stood. "Maggie wants to see you, Tom," he said then turned to Lacey. "And Lacey, you'll be sleeping in the cabin so when you two are done with supper we should go on up."

I pushed back from the table. "I'll put these dirty dishes into the wash water so the food won't dry out and stick. Then we'll go." I said eager to see Maggie.

But Eban put his hand on my shoulder. "I'll take care of the dishes, son," he said. "You finish eating. There ain't no hurry." And he left to collect the plates.

The grin on Lacey's face stretched as wide as the sky. Her eyes twinkled like when she first got here, like she was laughing at me again. "What?" I barked.

"Oh, I was just thinking. You're probably the only godfather in California whose britches are too short." She snickered again and covered her mouth with her hand.

But I knew my own eyes were even wider than hers. Maybe they even sparkled too. I couldn't tell. "Yeah, I guess I am," I said with my head held high. Right now I didn't care a fig about how short my pants were. I was a godfather.

##

Right above the tree line a golden moon glowed from a wash of stars. I waited for Eban on the hillside in front of Maggie's cabin. I'd just met little Josie Stone and my head spun like a top. Maggie had even let me hold Josie. Well, actually Maggie had to make me. Josie was so tiny. I feared I'd drop her and she would squash flat on the floor. But Lacey put her in my arms and when Josie stared back at me from brown eyes filled with trust, while a tiny trace of spit drooled down from the corner of her mouth, I knew how special this brand new baby girl must be.

Lacey took Josie back pretty quick. She seemed to like holding her and talked baby talk and played with Josie's little hands and stuff. Then she would rock Josie back and forth and hum real soft.

Maggie looked rough around the edges but had a warm glow about her that everybody talked about. I got the idea that having Josie was darn hard on her and so it must be a big relief now that it was over. Then Josie started fussing and Lacey shooed me out of the bedroom saying Maggie needed to feed her.

Eban had gone downstairs with me but ran into Mrs. Wimmer and now they jawed on the porch, but I went ahead to enjoy the night. I'd been cooped up in the cafe all day and the cool breeze mixed with the hoots from the owls that nested in the stable put me at ease.

Sitting on a hill like it did, the cabin had a great view. I could see the outline of Hangtown Creek where it ran beside Main Street at the bottom of the hill. On the south side of the road, just a little east of the log bridge, I could barely make out the stable and the freight office next to it, both partly hidden behind some tall oaks. A tad to the right of the bridge sat Maggie's Cafe, easy to see through a break in the trees.

Farther to the west stood the town, a little hard to make out in the dark but smoke rising from cooking fires marked it pretty well. Past the town the creek ran through a gully in a gap between the hills that on a clear day gave a glimpse deep into the great valley of California. The summer sunsets through that gap could be special.

I heard a door close and turned to see Eban heading down the stairs from the porch. It struck me how much he looked like my Pa. Both were stocky and had a bowlegged walk, but now Eban's hair had turned almost white while Pa only had a touch of gray when he died. It had been the resemblance that drew me to Eban on the first day we met. I hadn't thought about it much since.

He started talking as soon as he hit the bottom step. "Well, Tom, I guess we got kicked out of our beds. Are you going to be okay sleeping on the cot in the cafe?"

I hesitated a bit to mull over what he'd asked me. "Yeah, I guess so." I said finally. I didn't mind giving up my room to Lacey. I knew that was the gentlemanly thing to do. Besides, Eban let Mrs. Wimmer use his big feather bed in the dormer room upstairs next to Maggie and Joshua's so he had to sleep in the freight office. No, something else about Lacey sleeping in my bed made my insides feel jittery again, like they had when she grinned at me after Eban told me I was a godfather.

"Hey, sleeping in the cafe ain't that bad is it?" Eban must have noticed my mood.

"No, it's okay." I answered. "It's Lacey. She makes me feel funny, I guess."

"She's a pretty girl," he said. "And pretty girls can have a powerful pull on a young man like you, makes him think about getting married and raising a family."

"Getting married! I ain't thought about that none."

Eban grinned. "Ain't Josie the prettiest baby you ever saw? And with a ma as good-looking as Maggie and a pa as handsome as Joshua, she's going to grow up to be one eye-catching woman. You can bet your whole stake on that," he crowed, sounding real proud.

I'd never seen a newborn baby before, much less one as young as Josie, but I had seen some calves and a foal or two and even a day-old lamb once. They were all real cute, not pretty mind you, but cute. Now Josie was special, sure, but she only had a few ratty strands of brown hair on a head way too big and wrinkly skin as red as a beet. Maybe she would grow up to be pretty like Maggie but right now she had a long way to go.

I didn't answer Eban and we walked down the hill together in the dark.

At the log bridge he stopped. "Son, you and Lacey looked like you were getting along pretty good. Did she tell you anything about why she came to Coloma?"

"Not much, she said she rode up there looking for her Pa." I walked on few paces then turned back to face him. "Did she tell you anything, or maybe Mrs. Wimmer?" I asked, suddenly awful curious.

"A little, she came from San Francisco. Her Pa's named Webster Lawson. She's real scared something happened to him. After that she didn't want to talk about much. But three men turned up dead around Coloma in the last few weeks, two shot in the back, one beat to death, but Lacey's pa ain't one of them."

My face tightened. "Holy Moses, three guys dead, that's bad!" I said, knowing that fear had come into my eyes like it had to Lacey's earlier. One night last fall after Eban told me the men who murdered my brothers were chasing Maggie—I reckon 'cause she's so pretty—and he thought they might be in town, I swore I'd do anything I could to save her. In no time the scar-faced guy busted through the cabin door and shot Eban. I went after Scarface but he knocked me cold. Later, after I came to, Scarface and Joshua had at it. When Scarface shot Joshua I jumped in to help. Scarface near choked me dead, but I gave Joshua the time he needed to save our necks.

Eban smiled like he wasn't worried at all. "Take it easy, son. I don't think anybody's going to come looking for us this time," he said like he'd read my mind.

He'd almost died that night but Maggie dug the bullet out and saved him. I figured if Eban wasn't worried maybe I didn't need to be either, so I let out a long sigh. Now I could ask about what really bothered me.

"So Lacey came all the way from San Francisco? No wonder she knew about the roll-up pants they sell there," I blurted.

Eban chuckled. "Did she ride you about your trousers being short?"

"Yeah, she sure did! How'd you know that?"

"Women are like that, son, when they like a man." He looked toward the cafe. "Come on, let's heat up some coffee and I'll help you get the cafe squared away so you won't have to do it in the morning."

Walking across the bridge my mind wandered back to Lacey and her pa. "So why would Lacey come to the gold country all by herself to find her pa, Eban? Wouldn't she want to stay home with her ma like most gals do?"

Eban rubbed his chin like he always did when he thought. We stopped on the far side of the bridge to let a miner headed east ride by. "You know I spent time with Fremont's California Battalion during the war with Mexico, don't you?" he asked.

"I thought you and Joshua came here with General Kearny."

"After Fremont went south to fight the Mexicans he sent me east with Kit Carson. After we met Kearny on the trail we came back here with him. That's how I met Joshua."

I nodded, "Okay, but what's that got to do with Lacey?"

"I'll get to Lacey and her ma in a bit. First you need to hear the whole story. Fremont, with about fifty sharpshooters, came all the way across the country to map California, or so he said. When the Bear Flag Revolt happened and right after that the war with Mexico Fremont formed his battalion. I joined as a muleskinner, hauling stuff from here to there to get things set up for a new fighting unit. Those supplies got here way before the war, and Major Webster Lawson signed the shipping orders on everything I hauled. Sure as shooting, that's Lacey's pa."

"Holy Moses, if he was with Fremont then how did Lacey get out here?"

"Well, seems he wasn't with Fremont. He came on a ship from the east, way back in forty-five. They say his wife, that's Lacey's ma, died on that trip. Folks I know who saw him in San Francisco in the days before the war told me he didn't wear a uniform. He said he was an agent for a sailing company that wanted to build up business here in California, but those supplies we got came off whalers, ships headed for the fur trade up Oregon way and even ones that ran out to the Sandwich Islands and back. A lot of the provisions had been stored sometime way before most folks here had a whiff of an idea about a war with Mexico breaking out so soon."

"You mean to say that President Polk planned on having a war with Mexico?"

"That's what it looks like," Eban answered matter of fact like.

Together we stepped up onto the plank walkway in front of the cafe. "Gosh, Eban, does that mean Lacey's pa is some sort of spy or something?"

"No, not a spy, but he worked for the Army and he must have been sent here to help Fremont get the war supplies that couldn't be packed across the mountains. Bringing his family made the Major look like a civilian to the Mexicans. It could have been something the army did just in case, but there's folks who say the whole war was planned out just to get California into the union."

I pushed open the cafe's front door then held it for Eban to go in first. "So why did Major Lawson come to the gold country? There ain't no war here," I wondered.

Eban fired up a lamp. "I don't know," he said. "The last I

heard of Webster Lawson was almost two years ago. It's as much a puzzle to me as it is to you. I asked Lacey if her pa was in the army. She said he had been back in Washington."

While Eban lit another lamp in the kitchen, I tossed some kindling into the stove and put the pot on top. "Coffee'll be hot soon," I called.

"That's good." Eban said, his hands already elbow deep in wash water. "You'll be around Lacey a lot for a while. Maybe you can find out more from her. To tell the truth, something must have bothered that girl enough to take a whopping big risk coming up here like she did. And those murders in Coloma rub my hackles wrong for sure."

I grabbed a towel and began to dry. After what Eban said the fear I'd noticed lurking earlier in Lacey's eyes made sense. She must know something. Why else would she come so far alone? Maybe she would tell me. Maybe I could help find her pa.

2

A bright morning sun ambushed me as I walked out of the stable. I threw up a hand to block it and quickly turned west to put the glare behind me. Eban left early for Coloma with a wagonload of shovels and took Mrs. Wimmer with him. The last of our other wagons had pulled out for Sacramento City and I could still hear Woody Dunn yelling at the mules while the rig rolled down Main Street.

At the cafe I pushed open the back door, grabbed two oak pails from inside and toted them to the well where I filled them with fresh, cool water. Inside I tossed wood into the stove and started mixing up a batch of biscuits.

After I rolled out the dough the bell on the door jingled. It was way too early for customers so I kept working. Besides I thought it might be Lacey right off. She would come back here. I pulled out a biscuit cutter and started in on whacking out round hunks of dough and setting them onto a flat tin sheet. I'd almost filled it when she walked into the doorway.

"You're still the handiest boy around the kitchen I've ever seen."

I glanced up to see her leaning against the doorjamb again, her arms crossed in front of her chest. She looked a lot different than she did yesterday. It seemed like she'd tried to make herself homelier, but she was just naturally too pretty to pull that off. The pigtails did make her look younger. And her dress, one of Maggie's old ones, was faded and not as eye-catching as the yellow one, but she still filled it out real nice. I figured that somehow she looked a lot more winsome now that she didn't look so fetching.

"How's Maggie?" I asked, ignoring her barb about being handy in the kitchen.

"So you ask how Maggie is but you don't even care how I am," she shot back, her tone scruffy, like I'd riled her.

I didn't look up. "I know how you are. You're just as sassy as you were yesterday, but I haven't seen Maggie today and she's the one that just had a baby." I started sifting more flour for a second batch of biscuits.

"Maggie's doing fine and so is little Josie. We all had breakfast together," she said gently and I heard the soft pitter-patter of her footsteps coming toward me. "Is there something I can do to help?" she asked so downright sweet that it made my heart thump fast again.

I gazed into her deep blue eyes and smiled. "I'm glad you're here," I said. She broke a sheepish grin and looked down. She didn't say anything so I kept talking. "We need to get the dining room ready for lunch, make sure the tables are clean and the floor is swept up. It's Saturday and we'll be powerful busy most all day."

I thought Lacey would run right off to start sweeping but she stood there, twirling a finger in one of her pigtails.

I heard her gasp. "Maggie said you saved her life!" The words came out so fast the last one nearly tumbled over the first.

I grabbed the milk and slowly poured some into the bowl. I didn't want to answer her. I didn't know what to say. None of us ever wanted to talk about what happened that night.

She turned sideways, still playing with her hair. "I worried about it so much I couldn't sleep." She still talked way too fast, but seemed a little calmer.

I rolled up another ball of dough, wiped my hands on a towel and gave Lacey a small headshake and a big shrug. "It was no big deal." I said. "Any miner on Hangtown Creek would've helped Maggie then."

"Maggie wouldn't say anything about it either, but she told me that's why you're Josie's godfather." Lacey used the same scruffy tone she had earlier then took a deep breath. "Why won't you tell me?" she moaned and now her voice came across softer, more like a whine.

She had that big-eyed look about her too, like she had last night when Eban told me I was a godfather. And I had that same fluttery butterfly feeling jumbling up in my gut again, only strung a lot tighter now. I sprinkled a handful of flour on the cutting board and decided to change the subject. "Eban says you're looking for your pa. I know how you came to Coloma, but how did you get from San Francisco to Sacramento?"

"A man Papa knows gave me a ride in his boat." She sounded eager to talk about coming here. Maybe she would tell me something that could help find her pa.

"That was nice of him," I said, "but didn't you think that coming to the gold country would be dangerous—a young girl like you here with all these lonesome men?" I dumped the dough onto the floured cutting board a lot harder than I meant to. Maybe I was still a bit chafed at her for all the flirting she did with the customers yesterday.

"Mr. Flanagan told me that," she agreed. "He didn't want to bring me. I'd thought he might be hard to convince. That's why I wore my new dress and put my hair up and all. It's always easier to talk men into things when you look your best."

I sprinkled more flour over the dough ball. "I sailed across the bay with Shamus Flanagan once and he made that trip a whole lot of fun," I admitted. For some reason I was glad a man I knew had brought Lacey to Sacramento City, but I was still sore. "Is that what you were doing yesterday, looking pretty and trying to get men to do something for you?" I demanded, still feeling a little like I'd been taken advantage of.

I picked up the rolling pin and my eyes found hers. She had the sheepish grin across her face again but looked at me without a batting an eye and nodded. "I wanted you to feed me," she admitted. "I was so hungry. Then I thought somebody who ate here might know Papa and tell him where I was. Later, when you told me about being the only marrying age girl east of Sacramento City I got scared. Last night I asked Maggie about it. She said it would be best to not draw so much attention."

"Well, if somebody does know your pa he's bound to hear about you soon," I agreed. And with the rolling pin in both hands, I knocked the dough ball flat and pushed the pin over it first one way then another. "I can see how you got here easy enough, but why did you come in the first place? Ain't it dangerous for a woman to travel alone? Wasn't there somebody in San Francisco to take care of you?"

Her eyebrows scrunched together, dragging deep ruts into her forehead. "I was at home with Rosa, our housekeeper. But there's a man named Barkley who lives close by. He's ugly and mean and I hate him! I hate him!" She yelled, both fists pounding the table.

I dropped the rolling pin. "Lacey . . .?"

"I'm sorry. I'll be okay," she sighed and looked down at her trembling fists, her eyes wide, the glitter of tears covering her fear.

But she took a deep breath and kept talking. "He always tried to get me to go to his house. I was afraid of him. Then after Papa left he climbed through my window. He must've thought I was asleep. I wasn't. I screamed as loud as I could!" She sucked down another breath. "Rosa yelled back and that must have scared him. He swore he'd get me, then climbed back out the window laughing. I was terrified. I left the next day." She wiped her eyes and sniffled, but she didn't cry. Her hands shook but at least but she was talking now.

I didn't know what to say about this Barkley guy, but maybe she would tell me more about her pa. "You told Eban your pa wasn't in the army when you came to California, but Eban said that a Major Webster Lawson signed supply orders for Fremont's California battalion. That had to be your pa."

When I looked up her face had bleached whiter than the flour and her eyes bulged like she'd seen a will-o-the-wisp. "Does that mean my Papa is still in the army?" she whimpered.

"Yeah, it looks like he is," I went on, feeling like a rotten heel for causing her more grief. "Look, I reckon he was doing something meaningful here, but what did he do in Washington?"

She took a deep breath and calmed down some. "I don't know much, but I always thought what he did was important. He worked for General Scott—"

"Winfield Scott!" I exclaimed. "He won the war in Mexico!"

"Yeah, but that was after Papa came to California," she said then perked up. "Papa even had dinner at the White House sometimes. He knows President Polk and a lot of senators and congressmen. He'd take Mama and me to the park in our carriage on summer Sunday afternoons and all sorts of famous men would stop us just to say hello and maybe ask him a question. Mama said he would be a general soon."

Holy Moses, I thought. Lacey's pa really did sound like an important man.

"In San Francisco, after Mama died on the boat, I had to be the hostess when company came. I met Commodore Stockton and Governor Mason and even that young Lieutenant Sherman." She smiled wide and her eyes had a far off look in them.

When she mentioned that Sherman guy a bolt of jealousy struck my heart and I almost got riled again, but like lightning it faded fast. "Tomorrow's Sunday. The cafe's closed. We can get some horses from the stable and maybe ride around and look for your pa. Would you like that?" I tried my best to sound helpful but mostly I wanted to be with her somewhere outside the cafe.

Her eyes grew as big as hen's eggs. "Oh, yes! I'd love it! Can we, please, please?" She hopped up and down, flapping her arms like a chicken trying to fly.

"Sure we can. You can ride Maggie's chestnut. She won't be using him tomorrow anyhow. Maybe Eban will let me ride the dun. We'll go along the creek and talk to the miners. Somebody might know where we can find your pa."

"Yes, oh yes! You're wonderful." She stopped hopping and bolted around the table. Before I had a chance to duck she planted a sloppy, wet kiss on my left cheek and ran off. She grabbed the broom and disappeared into the dining room. In no time I heard a steady swish, swish, swish as she swept the floor.

I wiped my cheek with my palm and gave it a hard look for any sign of what Lacey had done to me. In spite of it all my face seemed fine, but when I picked up the rolling pin and started back in on the biscuit dough I realized I had no idea how to untie the knot that twisted up deep in my gut.

3

I bounded down the cabin steps two at a time, hopped on the dun and led the chestnut downhill toward the log bridge. I'd taken Lacey riding up the creek till near noon. We'd talked to a lot of miners, but no one had news of Webster Lawson.

Lacey said her pa left home weeks ago, but every day more and more men showed up here to mine and they found gold everywhere they went. The territory folks called gold country grew bigger and bigger. Web Lawson could be anywhere.

I dropped off Maggie's chestnut at the stable and rode towards town. Several miners had pointed out something that might help, a group called the California Mining Cooperative, the same bunch the man outside the Round Tent Saloon had talked about. It started in Coloma a while back and now they had an office here. A lot of miners went by there. Maybe Lacey's pa had too.

I saw the small sign hanging beside a staircase right past the Round Tent. One of the first businesses in town, the saloon still operated out of the same big tent it started in. They had a lot of customers too, especially on Saturday night and Sunday, and today was no different, but I still managed to find an open rail where I could tie the dun.

When I turned to climb the staircase a door at the top opened and a fellow came out. I recognized him as the same man who complimented my cooking the day Lacey showed up.

"How do you do, sir?" I called out while he locked the door. He must work here, I thought. I was in luck. "Are you with the mining cooperative?"

He put his key into a vest pocket and glared down the stairs at me before his face softened. "You're the boy from the cafe, aren't you?" he asked.

"Yes sir. I've been helping out there for a few days."

"Well, I'm pleased to see you again, son. I've heard a lot of good things about that cafe since I've been in town. Is there something I can do for you?" He started down the steps.

"Well, maybe, sir. I'm looking for a miner. His name is Webster Lawson and I wondered if you'd seen him."

The man stopped one step above the walkway so that I still had to look up at him. "It could be," he said without mulling things over much. "But I do see an awful lot of miners, and that name isn't familiar to me right off."

I craned my neck back to look into his eyes. "He's a tad taller than me, sir, and skinny." I said. "He wears a neat brown goatee with a thin moustache and has dark piercing eyes with really thick brows and a high forehead." I didn't know what dark piercing eyes meant exactly, but Lacey had told everybody we'd met today about her pa the same way so many times that I'd just repeated what she'd said.

"That could be a hundred men around here, but I've only been in town a few days now. You should check with our Coloma office. It's been open a lot longer," he offered.

"I guess I'll do that, sir. Thanks." I started to leave but the man called after me. I stopped and turned back.

"What's your name, son?" he asked.

He'd stepped down onto the plank walkway and I could look in his eyes easy now. "I'm Tom Marsh, sir." I held out a hand.

He took it and shook. "Pleased to know you, Tom. I'm Reid Harrison. When you do get to Coloma just tell my man there that I sent you. His name is Frank Barney. He's next to the Golden Nugget and he'll take good care of you."

The man still had a hold of my hand and for some reason I felt real uneasy so I pulled it away. I gave him an awkward wave as I took a step back. "I'll do that Mr. Harrison. Thanks a lot," I said as honestly as I could.

"Just call me Reid. Everybody does." He cracked a big smile and something about him put me more on edge. Maybe his missing front tooth made him look more like a brawler than the high-toned businessman he appeared to want folks to see him as. Then again it might have been something in his eyes that didn't play straight. I couldn't put a finger on it, but it seemed like he had too much oil in his words.

"Thanks again, Reid." I said and hurried back to the dun. While I untied the reins I watched him disappear inside the flap of the Round Tent Saloon. I remembered how he'd met Lacey in the doorway to the cafe Friday. He must've done something to her because she swatted at him with her purse. He'd ducked and went away laughing. And now, after I'd mulled it over, I'm sure I would've had the same fidgety feeling about Reid Harrison then except I'd been way too smitten by Lacey to think about anything else.

Horses were tied on each side of the dun so I backed him into the street to have more room to mount up, rubbing his neck as I did. I turned east toward the stable and grabbed the saddle, but just as my foot hit the stirrup a hand yanked my shoulder and spun me around. Before I could blink, a fist smashed into my left cheek exactly where Lacey kissed me yesterday. I tumbled backward into the dun's hindquarter. That caused him to bolt up the street and I landed on my rump in the dust.

"You lousy polecat," the hitter yelled. "Stay away from my gal or you'll get more of this than you can stomach."

I didn't recognize the voice right off so I shook my head to clear the cobwebs, but a boot caught me in the side. I grunted loud and rolled away. I found my feet, my mind fired up in a fine fettle, ready to fight, not about to abide anybody that sucker punched me in the face. I ducked a slow roundhouse blow aimed at my head, but I saw my attacker now—Jeremiah Wiggins who stank like an upturned whiskey still.

He let out a belch and wobbled some, almost toppling over. "Lacey's my gal," he slurred. "You stay away from her."

Wiggins didn't merely seem drunk, he looked totally stewed, three sheets to the wind. I took a step back. "Go home, Jeremiah, and sleep it off. You'll feel better tomorrow," I said. Though older and beefier than me, I still knew that liquored up like this I could take him easy.

"The hell you say!" He reached back and rolled out a long left hook that I stepped away from easy. I punched him hard in the jaw. He swore at me like the bully he was but he'd already had his chance. My time to repay him for what he'd given me had come. I hauled off and pounded him square in the nose as hard as I could. A loud oomph blew out of his mouth. He toppled clean off his feet, landed flat on his bum, blood spewing from his snout. He grabbed his sneezer with both hands and moaned.

I kept my dukes up and clenched, but hoped he would quit. "Stay down, Jeremiah. You're too drunk to fight," I warned, ready to smack him in the beak again if I had to.

Wiggins wiped at the blood with one sleeve, shook his head

and tried to push up with his other arm. It looked to me like he hadn't had enough, so I squared up to throw another right, just in case.

"Jeremiah, stop it!" The cry came from west of where I stood. I ventured a look. It was Jed Wiggins, heading this way at a full out gallop. Younger and smaller than Jeremiah and if push came to shove I thought I could take him, but I sure didn't want to fight both Wiggins' boys at the same time.

Without even a glance at me Jed raced up to his brother and pushed him back to the ground. He pulled off his yellow bandana and wiped it across his brother's bloody snoot. "Pa wants you back home right now," he yelled. "He's spitting more venom than an overheated rattler. You know how he gets when you drink like this." Then Jeremiah pushed Jed's hand away and mumbled something I couldn't quite make out.

It seemed like the fight was over so I glanced back over my shoulder for the dun. Eban's gray horse waited about fifty feet up the street. I backed up a step, ready to get out of here.

The motion must have caught Jed's eye and he looked over. "You go on, Tom," he said. "Jeremiah ain't going to fight no more. I'll take care of him. I'm sorry about this, but he just drinks too much sometimes, that's all." Jed shook his head, turned back to the drunken roughneck and yanked him to his feet.

While Jed struggled down the road, his brother draped over his shoulder, I saw how Jeremiah wore a pair of handmade Mexican boots like Reid Harrison had on. I noticed them at once because Jeremiah's dark blue pants were way too short and right in the middle of his rear end somebody sewed on a triangle shaped red patch that pointed straight down at them.

To me it seemed awful peculiar that a fellow would wear such high priced boots with homemade pants so badly mended. Still, I heaved a relieved sigh that the fight was over and trudged off to get the dun. He acted a bit skittish at first but calmed down when I stroked his neck and talked soft into his ear. My cheek ached some and when I wiped it with my hand a streak of blood showed up on my palm. Jeremiah's punch had cut me. There would be explaining to do when I got home.

I left the dun at the stable and walked down toward the log bridge. Past the freight office I glanced up the hill to the cabin. My gut growled from hunger, but I didn't want to answer all the questions I knew would come when everyone saw my face. Besides I needed to think so I headed for the cafe.

In the kitchen I built a fire under half a pot of coffee then stretched out on the cot and rubbed my side where Jeremiah kicked me. I ached some but it didn't seem like any serious harm came from the scuffle. Now I worried about any other love struck miner who might decide to fight me over Lacey, even though she wasn't even my girl or anybody else's for that matter.

She looked so fetching Friday. I could easily imagine every unmarried miner in Hangtown, and a lot of the married ones too, lining up to pop me in the face because of her. All at once she seemed a lot more dangerous than I'd ever dreamed a pretty girl could be. Still, I wanted to help her find her pa, even if I had to fight the whole town to do it.

But she had never told me why her pa came to the gold country. I'd always figured he wanted to mine. But when I thought about it, maybe there could be some other reason Webster Lawson left his beautiful young daughter alone in San Francisco to ride to the rough, unruly gold country—some really important reason that only an army officer could deal with. The trouble was Lacey had no idea about that. She didn't even know her pa was still in the army until I told her what Eban had said.

Then there was Reid Harrison and whatever seemed so bothersome about him. When he'd said he liked my cooking I'd taken a fancy to him at first. And today he acted real pleasant, downright sociable, yet something about him raised a pile of bafflement that gnawed deep inside my craw. But if Web Lawson didn't come here to mine he should have no interest in Reid Harrison's California Mining Cooperative. So I didn't rightly know what to think about anything that happened.

The coffee started to sizzle. It would come to a boil real quick and that would spoil the taste. With a groan I hopped up and rescued the pot from the stovetop, poured a cupful and put the pot back where it would stay warm and sat at the kitchen table.

The bell on the door rang about the same time I'd downed the coffee in my cup. I heard heavy boots thump on the dining room floor and Eban called, "Tom, you in the kitchen?"

"Yeah, Eban." Here it comes, I thought. He'll see my face and want to know what happened. I felt the cut on my cheek and sighed.

He stopped in the dining room doorway. "I saw the smoke from the stove and figured it was you," he walked to the table and pulled out a chair. "You plan on coming up for lunch? Lacey's making fried chicken and corn bread. I think she's doing it special for you."

"I went to town to talk to a man there. After that I came back here." I mumbled, worried now about why Lacey would want to cook for me. That made me even more edgy than the fight and I started to fidget. "There's still enough coffee left for both of us. Want some?" I asked, mostly to keep Eban from noticing my jitters.

"A cup of coffee would go nice right now," he answered.

I stood, filled both cups and handed one to him.

He took a small sip. "You been in a fight, Tom? Your face's cut."

I looked down to dodge his eyes. "Yeah, I got Sunday punched by Jeremiah Wiggins," I knew getting into a set-to with anyone but my brothers was downright disgraceful. I'd never done anything like it before.

"That's Doak Wiggins' oldest boy ain't it?" Eban asked without so much as a why so or what for.

"Yeah, I guess," I answered knowing I'd have to explain the fight to Eban, but somehow I'd still rather face a grizzly bear protecting her cub than talk about it.

"Well, if that's the only mark you got, you must've won," he said nice and easy.

I scrunched my mouth around as I recalled what happened. "He was drunk. I got lucky and hit him in the nose. That pretty much finished it," I took a sip of coffee, not so much because I wanted it but more because I still didn't want to face Eban.

"Folks say Jeremiah's got a fondness for the hard stuff." Eban went on. "Old Doak must hate it. He really walks the straight and narrow." He sat his cup on the table. "So what was Jeremiah's beef with you?" He pointed at me with his finger out and his thumb up, like a kid does when he pretends he has a pistol.

I glanced over toward the stove and sulked a bit, knowing this would be hard to talk about. "Oh, I don't know. Ask him," I said, hoping Eban would forget it.

"I'm asking you," he demanded, firm sounding but still gentle. He put his hands together, one palm flat against the other with his thumbs tucked in, like he was praying for an answer, or maybe for the right answer.

"Aw, Eban!" I whined and squirmed in my chair. I couldn't look at him face to face. The whole hoo-ha embarrassed me too much. Me, fighting with a drunk in the middle of the street on a Sunday afternoon, my pa would never have put up with it. But I had to tell him something, and it had to be the truth. "He says Lacey's his girl. He wants me to stay away from her."

Eban picked his coffee cup up again. "A pretty girl like Lacey can cause a peck of trouble among young men your age. That's the gospel truth."

For the first time I dared to peek at him. He didn't smile exactly but he sure didn't frown either. He had a faraway look, like he was chewing over some dark secret or maybe remembering something from a long time ago. Leastwise he didn't seem mad at me for fighting Jeremiah and I felt a powerful sense of relief.

But now that Eban knew about the fight, I wanted to make sure he knew the meat and potatoes of it. "Jeremiah had been drinking something fierce. He could hardly stand up. He Sunday punched me when I started to mount the dun. I didn't hit him hard but once and he flopped over like he'd slipped in bacon fat."

Eban's eyes snapped back into the here and now and he chuckled. A grin spread across his face, too big to be caused by what I'd just told him. "Yes sir, a pretty girl sure can get a man into a rumpus so big there ain't no possible way to wiggle out," he said and from the look that went with the grin maybe Eban had been remembering. "I reckon you'd best come up with a better story for Maggie though," he went on. "She ain't going to cotton to you scrapping in the street. Could be the dun kicked you, I suppose?"

Now I took my turn to smile. Eban had made light of my scuffle and wanted to help keep it from Maggie. "Okay, if she asks I'll tell her I got kicked. She'll believe that." In a way I felt a heap better now. Eban could make something real serious look like just a part of the everyday way. So maybe he would do the same with my other imponderable. "Have you heard of a place called the California Miner's Cooperative? It's run by a man named Reid Harrison?"

"Reid Harrison?" Eban blurted the name out real loud and scratched his chin whiskers. "I ain't sure but that might be a guy I knew of during the war. But I did hear talk about how the mining cooperative is a way for new miners to hedge their bets if they ain't sure what they can do here. They all pool together the gold they mine and split the pot every so often. Maybe I heard wrong cause in any situation like that there's bound to be those what don't pull their share. I'll look into this Harrison feller for you though. Probably he ain't the same guy I'm thinking of."

"Thanks, Eban. I've seen him a couple of times and he leaves me feeling like I'm stepping in fresh horse leavings. It might be nothing, but when I asked him about Lacey's pa he said to see a man in Coloma. How about I take a wagon over in the morning?" I asked, already feeling a lot better after Eban came down on my side.

"Hallelujah! You're welcome to it." he grinned wide then stood up. "Let's you and me walk up to the cabin. The women folk are looking to see you."

"All right Eban. I'll go," I said. Talking to Eban had helped boost my frame of mind a lot.

4

"Easy mules, whoa now!" I pulled hard on the brake lever to keep the heavy wagon from rolling out of control down the hill. Off to the left huge redwoods towered high above the road, but to the right the ground fell off into a blanket of brambles and brush covered by a thick stand of pine. The air here had a clammy smell, even in summer. Not far ahead ran the American River, another sharp turn and I would be in Coloma.

I'd left home way before sunup so I would have more time to look up this Frank Barney fellow at the California Mining Cooperative and ask him about Lacey's pa. I was used to the early mornings. For a month or more before Maggie had little Josie I did the same thing every day so I could make it back to the cafe early enough to give her a hand with the noon rush.

I caught a quick glimpse of the river ahead flashing through the trees. The trail took a hard turn to the left. "Haw Mules, haw here. Come on now, haw!" I pulled hard on the reins. The two lead mules did as I wanted and in no time the wagon rolled into the boomtown of Coloma.

It knocked me off my feet at how fast the town had grown. When I first got here this time last year there were only a handful of shops. Now Coloma had become a dyed-in-the-wool city, with hundreds of buildings bustling with shopkeepers and miners. The saw mill lay ahead, tucked inside a big loop in the river, with piles of fresh cut lumber in its lot.

I passed the Golden Nugget Saloon and saw the sign for the California Miners Cooperative hanging near a staircase that led up beside the butcher shop next door. I knew the saloon well, too well maybe. I'd worked there last year, cleaning out the place in the mornings. It had been a hard summer. Things were much better now.

"Gee mules. Gee now," I hollered and pulled the team to the right, into the saw mill yard and up beside a stack of planks. When the rig rolled to a stop I tugged on the hand brake, threw a loop over it and hopped to the ground.

"Load your wagon, mister, only a dollar." Every time I came here someone ran up wanting work. A year ago it might have been me yelling those words in hopes of making a little money for food. Coloma could be a hard place for a young boy alone. But it was right in this very lot that I'd first met Eban, and by that evening I'd met Maggie. It had been the luckiest day of my life.

I recognized the speaker at once. "Hi, Boyd, how've you been?" I said. Maybe eighteen or so, tall and skinny, Boyd Riddle hustled toward the wagon with a gawky lope, bobbing his head and swinging his arms wide. I liked him a lot. Dressed like a farmer from head to toe, what you saw is what you got with Boyd.

"Morning, Tom, I been fine. Pa's near healed up. We'll be back mining soon."

"That's good news. I wish you the best. Remember, if things don't work out you can always come and see me. The freight line is growing steady. We'll find work for you." I liked helping people who needed it, like Eban helped me once.

"That's mighty charitable of you, Tom, but I got to stay with Pa. You understand." Boyd stopped walking and, with one hand on his hip, drew in a deep breath.

"I understand," I said. "Look, I've got some things to take care of. How about I give you two dollars and you load the whole pile?" It was a good deal and I knew it, but I also knew some things about why Boyd wanted to load wagons. His pa busted a leg and fell into Weber Creek a few weeks back. Boyd pulled him out of the water and hauled him into town for help. Now he did anything he could to get food for both of them.

"Sure, Tom, thank you. Thank you kindly," he beamed a wide grin across his freckled face. I knew that the extra dollar would come in handy.

"I'll be back as soon as I can." I said and stuck out my hand. Boyd shook it and I walked off towards town.

A steady clang of iron on iron rang out as I passed the blacksmith shop along Coloma's dusty main road at the edge of the saw mill lot. The Golden Nugget sat across the street and a few doors to the east. At the top of the stairs by the butcher shop I found the door to the mining cooperative open so I walked right in.

The room had only a few chairs scattered around the walls and a lone table over by the back wall. The same guy Reid Harrison had been with at the cafe, the one with the pudgy face and bushy eyebrows, sat behind it working on a pile of papers.

He looked up when I stepped inside. "Can I help you?" he asked.

The man sounded gruff, like I wasted his time. The same uneasy feeling I'd had with Reid Harrison rose up in my gut, and in the blink of an eye I made up my mind. "Sorry to bother you, sir. I came here with my Pa a while back. He got hurt but he's feeling better now and ready to mine. We been hearing about the mining cooperative so I came by to see what we got to do to join up," I lied, plain out and bald faced.

The man stood and his grumpy look melted a bit. "Well, I'd be happy to help you, son," he said and held out a hand. "I'm Frank Barney. I run this office."

I took his hand and shook it. "Pleased to meet you, Mr. Barney, I'm Boyd Riddle."

"Call me Frank," he said in a voice that seemed as oily as Reid Harrison's. "Have a seat." He waved at an empty chair across the table. "You came to the right place. We got plenty of good claims that need miners. I'll have you working in no time."

I sat, thankful for a chance to look down, sure that the lie I'd told Frank Barney was plastered across my face like mud on a pig, and fully expecting to be called out for it anytime. I didn't have much practice at this sort of thing, even though yesterday, when I'd told Maggie the dun kicked me, I'd done it mostly to keep her from worrying about me fighting with Jeremiah Wiggins. But now I'd told a dirty rotten whopper from top to bottom without even knowing why I'd done it.

Frank Barney pushed aside the papers he'd been working on and folded his arms over the table. "The mining cooperative is easy to join. You just sign up and you're in. That's it. We have some of the best claims in the gold country and our miners average five to six dollars a day. That's real good money, you know," he bragged.

Already in up to my eyeballs I had to keep up my story, so I tried to act like a guy fresh from the farm. Fortunately it hadn't been that long ago since I lived on one. "Shucks sir, that sure sounds pretty good to me. I reckon Pa would think so too." I jumped in with both feet and stared directly into Frank Barney's eyes. "But I talked to a fellow yesterday—named Lawson, I think—do you know him?" I asked.

Frank Barney didn't bat a lash. "That name don't ring a bell," he said firmly.

"Well, I ain't real good with names. It could've been Lawton or Lawless or some other. Anyhow, the fellow said that since you split the money among all the miners some folks would get lazy and not work as hard as others. Is that true?"

Frank Barney's hand slapped the table hard, his face red. "No! That's nothing but a lie," he bellowed. "Anybody don't work don't get paid. We got all kinds of safeguards. Men work in teams and we rotate them so folks can't make backdoor deals. We run cheats right out of this cooperative. Anybody say's our guys don't work is lying, plain lying!"

He talked about people lying way louder than somebody ought to and I wondered if he'd figured out I lied too. Still, I went along like everything was on the up and up. "That's right good to hear, Frank," I declared. "My Pa sure don't like paying the way for dawdlers. He's real determined that everybody work for what they get. He'll be happy to hear you ain't got none of that stuff here."

"I run a tight ship out of this office," he growled. "I'll fight any man who say's different. You can tell that to your pa," Frank Barney still sounded steamed.

I stood. "I'll sure tell him, sir," I promised, lying through my teeth. "We'll be back as soon as Pa's up to it. Thanks for your time." I eased behind my chair.

"You do that son. You come back anytime. I'll get you set up and working a gold bearing claim faster than you can shake a stick. No use panning all over the place looking for color." Barney stood too. He'd calmed down a bit and wasn't yelling anymore.

"Pa'll like that. We could use the money," I said and headed for the door. I looked back as I opened it, and then touched the brim of my blue army forage cap. I figured it sort of a goodbye salute. I didn't plan on seeing Frank again.

"You be sure to come back, you hear," he said, looking a lot like Pa did when he'd stand over the kitchen table and bark orders to my brothers and me back on the farm.

"You can count on it, sir." I ducked through the door and quickly pulled it shut behind me. At the top of the stairs I paused long enough to grab a deep breath and mop the sweat from my forehead with my sleeve. Somehow I didn't think Frank Barney had figured out I'd lied. But inside I knew there was something awful wrong with what I'd just done, yet the whole underhanded story had simply slipped out of my mouth. When I was younger and told only a tiny fib Pa would always take a hickory stick to my backside.

I hotfooted it down the stairs and into the street, dodging two horses and a small wagon as I scurried across. Through the open door of the blacksmith shop flurries of orange sparks flew from a red-hot hunk of metal each time the smith pounded on it. When I rounded the corner of the smithy, Boyd Riddle still worked hard to load the pile of planks into the back of the freight wagon and had a good ways to go yet. I'd already agreed to give him more money to do the whole job himself so I spun and marched back down the main street of Coloma.

In front of a large, many-paned glass window at P. T. Burns General Merchandise I stopped, and there, hanging over a sawhorse, I saw three pairs of roll-up pants, one each in black, brown, and blue, just like the ones Lacey had talked about. In no time the bell over P. T. Burns' door jingled loud when I pushed my way inside.

In my whole life I'd never bought new clothes before, never worn anything but hand-me-downs, so maybe I did get a little carried away. Mr. Burns had four satisfied customers come and go before the bell over the front door rang again on my way out. I wore a brand new blue work shirt and a shiny new pair of black roll-up pants. Under my arm, wrapped in brown paper tied with twine, I carried both the blue and brown pants as well as two more work shirts, one each in tan and dark green.

When I rounded the smithy once more and walked into the saw mill lot, I saw Boyd still hard at it but now nearly done loading the pile of lumber. A large pang of guilt jittered down my spine. I'd lied to Frank Barney and used Boyd's name. Somehow I didn't much care how Frank felt about it, but if Boyd and his pa went into the mining cooperative office and tried to sign up things might get troublesome. I sure didn't want either of them hurt because of me.

"Hi Boyd," I said. "I see you're about done here." I walked by him and tossed the brown paper bundle onto the driver's bench. When I looked back he'd stopped working and stared at me with his mouth wide open, still holding a plank twenty feet long and as thick as my thumb.

"Now don't you look pretty all dressed up in brand new store bought clothes like that?" he gushed. "I do declare, I never seen the like on nobody I knew before now."

Boyd's bootlicking rubbed me right and I couldn't help a

boastful grin. "Well, they were ragging me about my pants being short so I had to do something." I admitted while I headed to the lumber pile to grab another board.

Meantime Boyd heaved the plank in his hands onto the wagon and took the other end of the one I pulled on. "I ain't never worried about my britches being short," he said. "Long as they fit my middle that's fine."

"It's a first for me too," I agreed. "When you hit a big strike on one of these creeks around here you'll be able to get some store-boughts yourself." And together we slid the board onto the wagon.

Boyd grinned, "I 'spect I'll do that. Can't hurt none."

We picked up another board together. That left only one more. I decided the time had come to ask Boyd the question that nagged me since I'd talked to Frank Barney. "Have you heard of the California Mining Cooperative, Boyd?"

"Ain't that them fellers that put all the gold they've mined in a pot and then split it up equal like?"

"That's them."

"Yeah, a feller who must've been staying nearby stopped at our camp once. He told me that outfit runs Mexican and Chinese miners off good claims so they can put their guys onto them. Don't know if that's a fact but I've heard more talk about shenanigans going on there." We packed the heavy board onto the wagon and turned to the last plank. "Pa's too ornery to work with any of them fresh off the boat city folks anyhow," Boyd went on.

My guilty mind eased some because of what he'd just said. If something bad happened to a nice guy like Boyd because I'd used his name in talking to Frank Barney I knew I'd have a hard time living with it. And I still couldn't forget how my Pa wouldn't cotton to a man who lied.

After paying Boyd his two dollars I climbed up on the wagon bench, let off the brake and cracked the reins. In no time the rig rolled out of Coloma and started up the hill. I pushed the mules as hard as I dared, eager to get home, and not because I had cooking to do in the cafe. It was closed today. I wanted to see Lacey and show off my new pants. Maybe she would like them.

Heading back up the hill meant hard work for me as well as for the mules. Because of the weight of the lumber the whole run back home from the saw mill put way more strain on the team. I had to keep them moving by yelling a lot and cracking the reins. If they stopped going uphill it could be hard to get the heavy wagon rolling again.

When I finally reached the top I let the mules go at a pace they felt comfortable with, sort of a walking rest for them. It gave me a chance to relax some too. I wanted to moon a while over Lacey and how she would gush when she saw my new roll-up pants, but instead my mind kept wandering back to Frank Barney.

A lot of things shuffled around in my head, like how quick Frank said he didn't know Lacey's Pa. Anybody hearing a name he didn't recollect a face with right off should take some time to ponder it before he answered. At worst, since Frank sat right in his own office, he might've offered to check his paperwork to see if he had the name Lawson somewhere. No, it sort of sounded like he knew the name but said he didn't.

Then there's how mad Frank got when I brought up the stuff about miners shillyshallying around and still getting a share of the gold other men mined. His face burned as red as the back end of a strawberry roan and in no time flat too. I would've thought that if things went as good as Frank wanted me to believe he'd be proud of that and would do more crowing than squawking.

But what Boyd Riddle said burdened my thoughts most. Boyd hadn't been in Coloma long, didn't have much schooling but seemed pretty much a straight shooter. Boyd and his Pa were probably a lot alike, neither one liked anybody who sat on his butt and didn't carry his fair share of the load. No farmer did. But Boyd talked matter of fact about hanky-panky with the mining cooperative. That kind of tomfoolery would be from Frank Barney and Reid Harrison as far as I knew. It sure seemed like they weren't on the up and up somehow.

Still they could be the biggest hornswogglers in the world but that would be a problem for the sheriff to dig into, not the army. If Frank Barney and Reid Harrison had anything to do with Lacey's pa why they did stayed a total puzzlement to me. No matter what kind of scoundrels these two might be, there still seemed no reason for Webster Lawson to get mixed up with them. Yet, like Eban would say, if I had to bet on it, I'd be betting that all three knew each other somehow, and knew each other real good.

The wagon picked up speed when it started down the hill. I grabbed the brake and pulled, slowing the headway of the heavy load and easing the strain on the team. I gently tugged on the reins to bring the mules back to a walk. I had a long way yet to go. The hill got steeper closer to town. I needed to keep a lid on the pace of things with so much weight. If things got out of control, the wagon could upend real easy, spilling the lumber and maybe doing harm to both the animals and me. I pulled off my blue army hat and put it on the seat to let what little breeze that blew here cool my sweaty forehead. I'd finished ruminating on the mining cooperative for now.

I heard the speedy clip-clop of a horse coming hard from behind. Men didn't often ride fast along this stretch. Maybe there was trouble. I turned and watched a fellow in a red shirt and wearing a dirty white straw hat with a blue bandana around his neck ride up. He didn't look much like a miner. When he reached the wagon he slowed to a walk and stared at me from eyes as cold as a Sierra blizzard before he sped on without even a how-do.

Somehow, even on such a hot day, a chill crept down my spine. The fellow stopped on the trail ahead and turned his horse. He eyeballed me again, causing me sizable consternation before he spun his pinto and tore off. I didn't like guns much, never had, but right now I wished I had one. In all the trips I'd made to Coloma and back along this same road I'd never met anybody so unsociable, so downright scary, as this guy in the red shirt. Only half way home, all alone and without any help, I picked up my cap and pulled it tight on my head, somehow hoping an army hat might save me from harm.

But the rig still headed down a long hill and I had to work the brake, pull on the reins and zigzag the wagon to keep the speed down. For a while I forgot about both the guy in the red shirt and Frank Barney. At last, through the trees, I could see the roofs of the town ahead. I'd nearly made it back to Hangtown, and Lacey Lawson. Hangtown Creek lay at the bottom of the hill only a few hundred paces away. The bank on the far side of the stream was the last real rise before Main Street. With the danger of upending the load almost gone a little speed would help the heavy wagon get up that bank.

I leaned in to snap the reins over the mules when I heard a loud crack from somewhere in front. My blue army cap suddenly blew away. A burning hot pain seared the top of my head. A gunshot! Somebody shot at me. I had no idea who, but the guy in the red shirt came to mind. I dropped the reins and leaped from the wagon.

My feet hit the ground. I rolled over and quickly curled in

behind a sugar pine. I stared down the trail. About fifty feet away my wagon bounced over ruts and roots as it gained speed. And right there a puff of gray gun smoke hung in the air. The shooter had to be somewhere close to that smoke. I kept my eyes peeled.

A man with a rifle in his hand and a big red triangle shaped patch on the seat of his pants leaped out of the woods at a dead run and followed the wagon until they were both out of sight. I couldn't be pure positive but I'd bet my brand new roll-up pants that Jeremiah Wiggins shot me. Unfortunately my pants still sat on the driver's seat of the run-away wagon.

Now that the shooter left I figured I could walk the short way to town. But when I stood I got dizzy right off. I rubbed my scalp. Hot blood covered my palm. My mind went groggy. My knees turned wobbly. I slumped against the tree. My head thumped and swirled around. I teetered on the edge of a dark hole . . .

##

"Tom! Tom, answer me. Do you hear me? Tom!"

Somebody called my name, a hollow voice from somewhere far off that echoed inside my head like a drum pounding from deep down a well. I wished they would go away and leave me alone.

I could see Lacey, so pretty in her yellow dress, her hair in pigtails, dancing, spinning across a field of flowers. I ran after her, fast like the wind, but she soared high over the ground, her dress framed against the deep blue sky.

"Tom! Wake up Tom!"

The hollow voice barged into my happiness again. Why won't they let me be, I thought? I had to catch Lacey, so I soared into the sky behind her, closer and closer I came. Free, like a falcon, I followed her every move through the small puffs of cloud that floated by.

She turned and spread her hands wide, beckoning to me, waiting for me. I flew into her open arms and hugged her, happy, content. But the next thing I knew she'd disappeared, crumbled to pieces like a sugar cookie under a heavy boot.

I grasped desperately at the empty air for any shred of her, but found nothing. Lacey had vanished. Gone! And I was falling, tumbling faster and faster. The ground rushed up to meet me, the field of flowers now hard, jagged rock. I smashed into it.

My head hurt, bad. I moaned, long and low.

"Tom, you awake?"

Someone called me. It sounded like someone I knew. I smelled whiskey.

"Take it easy, son, you'll be all right."

How could I be all right? Lacey had disappeared. "Ooooh." I groaned. Then something wet ran onto the top of my head. "Youch!" It stung! A lot! Whiskey! Someone poured whiskey on my head. My eyes popped open. "That hurts!" I whined.

"Well, it's about time you came around. I was worried." Eban crouched over me with an open bottle and a bloody bandana in his hand.

"Where's Lacey?" I looked around for her but everything seemed blurred. I wiped the sweat from my eyes with the sleeve of my new blue shirt. It helped.

"Take it easy," Eban said. "Lacey's fine. She's back at the cabin with Maggie. But what happened to you? Do you remember? Did you see who shot you?" Worry oozed from his voice. I'd never heard him sound so fretful.

"Shot me?" What Eban said dumbfounded me. Did someone shoot me? A recollection of Jeremiah running away popped into my mind. "Oh, no," I moaned, something had happened. "I need to think." I mumbled, groggy, my head still in a cloud. Why was I sitting under this pine tree on the trail to town? Did Jeremiah really shoot me? Why would he do that?

"Maybe this will spur your remembering a bit." Eban walked to the dun, grazing on tall grass just a few feet away. He pulled something from his bags and waved it at me. "Here's your cap," he said. "It was in the back of the wagon." He stuck his finger through a hole in the top. "The shot went right through it. You're lucky you ain't dead."

He held the cap out. I took it and stared a while before I slowly put a hand on my head. I felt the scab forming where the ball had grazed my scalp. If I hadn't ducked to whip the reins the shot would have hit me square in the face. I'd be dead. I gulped. It was the scariest thought I'd ever had.

"It was Jeremiah Wiggins—least I think it was." I pointed down the trail. "He was right there by the big gnarled pine. I saw him run off before I passed out."

Eban grimaced. "The mules came back to the stable," he told

me. "I saw the rig pass the freight office and went after it. Obadiah must've figured something was up. He had the dun saddled when I got there. There was a package on the wagon seat, shirts and trousers. They yours?"

The news that I hadn't lost my new pants was small comfort now. The whole stickler boiled down to why Jeremiah Wiggins wanted to shoot me over a bout of fisticuffs. Did he want Lacey enough to kill for her? That plain didn't make sense. I hunkered down and clutched the cap tight to my chest, shivering like a spring sapling in a strong winter wind. "I don't understand, Eban. Why would anybody shoot me?"

Eban bent over and felt through my hair. I winced when he hit the wound. "You're awful lucky," he repeated. "But we need to get you back to town if you're up to it."

Though I still felt a whole bunch under the weather I wanted to get out of here bad. "I guess I'm okay. Are we riding double?"

"Yeah, but I want you sitting in the front so I can hang on to you. Getting hit in the head can do funny things to a man." Eban took my arm, pulled me to my feet and helped me into the saddle.

We crossed the creek and turned left on Main Street. Up at the Round Tent Saloon a couple of men come out of the tent flap bickering like folks do who know each other—Jeremiah Wiggins and the man in the red shirt. Even from two stores down the street I saw Jeremiah's jaw drop when he noticed me. Right off he ducked back inside the saloon. But Red Shirt calmly lit a cigar and scowled while we rode by.

I felt Eban turn back to look. He must have spotted Jeremiah with the red shirt guy too. I nudged the dun so he'd go faster. Seeing Jeremiah with the same fellow that eyeballed me up and down on the trail with an ice-cold glare and not even a simple how do you do caused me to break out in a bad case of the shudders.

At the cafe I pulled up. Eban hopped to the ground first. I slid down off the saddle slow and easy so as to not aggravate the thumping in my head. I wobbled while crossing the plank walkway. At the cafe door I looked back at the dun.

Eban had the reins in his hand. "Make sure both doors are latched," he ordered. "Don't let nobody in you don't know. I'll be back soon. Meantime you rest."

"Okay, Eban," I waited until he rode off toward town before I went inside, threw the latch and walked to the kitchen where I crawled right onto the cot. Eban was right. I needed rest. Things had started to spin again, around and around.

After a while the whirling slowed but I still had a throbbing ache that kept me from getting full at ease. I needed to sort out what happened today but couldn't fix my thoughts on any one thing. My mind seemed like Maggie's deer meat stew—a lot of little pieces of different stuff mixed together.

Finally I tried to sleep. That didn't work either but I found that if I lay quiet and only thought about breathing deep and slow I felt better, even the pounding in my head calmed down. I closed my eyes and managed to rest a while. Then a loud knock at the back door jarred me to the here and now.

The rap came again, louder. The door pushed in. My head jerked up. I moaned.

"Tom, I told you to latch both doors!" It was Eban, yelling, sounding awful mad. But I closed my eyes again and with a deep sigh eased back against the pillow. I'd forgotten to latch the back door but now I was glad. I didn't want to get up.

Eban rumbled around the kitchen. I heard a heavy thump on the table then a lighter one. "I reckon it's my fault," he said, his voice softer. "I know what can happen when a man gets hit in the head. I should've come in with you. But no harm done."

I heard his footsteps cross to the cot. I opened my eyes.

He held out a hand with small pistol in it. "Put this in your pocket," he said.

I took the gun. "This is Maggie's." I blurted and looked up at him. "Why Maggie's gun? Does she know?" I was in a world of trouble now but didn't want Maggie to worry about me. She had enough to do with little Josie and all.

He exhaled through his lips with a breathy whistle. "Well, it's going to be hard to keep it from her, but for now I reckon we can say you fell off the wagon and hit your head. Sooner or later she's bound to hear different. Anyhow, she gave the gun to Joshua, said she didn't want it anymore."

I frowned. "I know there's lots she don't talk about, bad things must've happened to her, but I don't want to add to that by bringing more trouble down on us." I stuffed the small pistol into my pants pocket. I still didn't like guns much and didn't feel easy with the idea of shooting Jeremiah Wiggins, or anybody else, but having it handy was a comfort now.

Eban pointed at the pocket, his face stern. "You know how to use it don't you?"

I gave him a tiny nod. "Yeah, I guess so."

"Remember, you only got one shot. Don't waste it. You can't shoot far and hit anything with this gun. It's made for close up shooting. Best is to stick it right into somebody's gut before you pull the trigger." He turned back to the table. "I brought you this too." He held it up a double-barreled shotgun. "There ain't nothing that puts the fear of God into a varmint like a scattergun. A man don't even have to be much of a shot to hit what he's aiming at. You point this around and any right thinking polecat's liable to back off."

I scrunched up my mouth, gloomy, worried. "I ain't never shot nobody," I said.

"I understand, son. No decent man wants to shoot another one, but it's best to be ready. There's lots of folk around that ain't decent. Looks like you ran into one."

"Yeah, I guess I did." The whole thing scared me. I didn't like the idea that somebody tried to kill me. I didn't like it one bit.

All at once Eban smiled, a genuine tooth flashing grin. "I got you one more thing," he put the shotgun back on the table and picked up a wide-brimmed, Mexican straw sombrero. "I figured you needed some new head gear and this one might throw Jeremiah Wiggins off your scent at least once. The rascal might mistake you for one of them Mexican fellers."

I cracked a small smile for the first time since the shooting, swung my legs over the side so I could sit on edge of the cot, tossed the shot up army cap onto the table and put the sombrero on. "Arriba!" I said with a bit of spunk, and even circled a forefinger above my head like the Mexican vaqueros did.

My reaction to the hat brought a chuckle from Eban. "I'm glad you like it, Tom. It looks good on you." His face turned serious again. "Do you know the man in the red shirt who came out of the Round Tent Saloon with Jeremiah Wiggins?"

"No, I never saw him till today. He tore up behind me on the trail from Coloma, slowed to a walk and glared at me a while before galloping off like I had the cholera or something."

"Ain't many who ride fast on that trail—unless it's life or death important. But nobody I talked to in town knew him either, nobody but Jeremiah Wiggins, I reckon."

"There's something else funny, Eban." I replied. "I talked to a fellow named Frank Barney in Coloma. He's Reid Harrison's partner. He said he doesn't know Lacey's pa either, but he said it so fast, without pondering on it, that I'd bet they both know him."

Worry lines wrinkled across Eban's forehead. He pulled a chair from the table and sat down with his arms folded on top of the backrest and faced me. "Let's say you're right and there's some bad blood between Webster Lawson and them two varmints. Suppose the one in Coloma knew you were looking for Lacey's pa and sent the guy in the red shirt back to tell this Reid Harrison feller."

Eban made sense, but a lot of stuff that I couldn't wrap my mind around still needed answers. I hoped Eban could help. "Maybe so," I said. "But the guy in the red shirt wasn't with Reid Harrison. He was with Jeremiah and Jeremiah did the shooting."

"Well, to me it looked like those two were squabbling. They might've just met in the saloon and got under each other's skin is all. Jeremiah likely shot at you on account of Lacey. Folks say he's laid his claim to her and you're in his way."

"Ain't shooting somebody just to get a girl going way too far?" I barked the words, loud, mean. The sudden rage caught me short. It had come out of the blue.

Eban's eyebrows rose. His jaw dropped. He grabbed his chin like he did when he pondered things. "For sure it's going too far," he agreed, sounding real understanding. "But Jeremiah's been hitting the likker hard lately."

I shrugged and shook my head. "I don't know. Something ain't adding up like it ought to." I'd calmed down a little. Yelling made my head hurt.

"Right now the important thing is to keep you safe," Eban said. "I'll take the wagon to Coloma in the morning, check on things. Maggie's talking about coming back to work here tomorrow. With Lacey helping out she thinks she can handle it. You take a day off. Stay at the cabin and let that head settle down."

A loud pounding came from the front door. "Tom, I know you're in there. Let me in. Right now!" Lacey sounded as mad as a cat in the rain.

Eban broke into another toothy grin. "Hold your horses, Lacey. I'm coming," he hollered. He picked up the shotgun and leaned it against the wall by the cot, all the while looking right into my eyes. "And if you was thinking getting shot at was the worst thing that ever happened to you, you was wrong. You're about to get a taste of the most perplexing vexation a man can have. Welcome to woman trouble, son. I think you got a big portion coming."

While Eban walked to the door, I reflected back on Lacey, and how I'd bought the new pants earlier in Coloma for her. I remembered how much I wanted to please her, but that was before Jeremiah shot at me. That seemed a long time ago now. I took off the sombrero and eased back onto the cot.

The bell over the door jingled and somebody talked in low tones. I took a deep breath. She'd be here in no time.

Then Lacey yelled, louder than I'd ever heard her. "Tom fell out of the wagon! Oh Lord! Is he hurt?"

"Lacey, calm down, he's okay." Eban said.

She stopped in the doorway, wearing her yellow dress, her hair in pigtails. "Tom Marsh, how dare you get yourself hurt and not tell me." The corners of her mouth drooped so low I thought they might fall off her face. She looked all out of sorts and it seemed to me she thought it my fault she felt so miserable.

I wanted to explain so she would feel better. "I didn't want to bother you—"

"Bother me! How could you ever think such a thing?" She sniffled and dabbed her eye with a handkerchief.

"But I was dizzy and—"

"Dizzy! You mean you hit your head when you fell?"

"Well, yeah." I said without thinking. She was the second person I'd lied to today. Lying was becoming a bad habit, but I just couldn't tell her I'd been shot.

"Oh, you poor man!" She rushed toward me like a hungry calf after its ma.

Behind her I could see Eban, framed by the door and grinning like a fox that caught a baby chick. The woman trouble Eban warned me about had hit me full bore. First Lacey got mad at me. Now she wanted to take care of me. Holy Moses, I thought, what will happen next?

She reached the cot and loomed over me like a mother duck. I scrunched back into the bed and wondered how somebody so soft and gentle looking could seem so fearful sometimes. She fluffed up a pillow, slipped her hand behind my neck and pulled up, stuffing the pillow beneath my head.

"Yeee-ooow!" I yelled. The pain pounded through my shot-up noggin.

Her hand flew up to cover her wide-open mouth. "I'm sorry! Did I hurt you much?" she whimpered from under her fingers.

My eyes closed. The throbbing thumped hard behind them. I breathed slow and steady like I had earlier and the pounding eased pretty quick. Lacey sounded real sorry that she hurt me. I knew she wanted to help, but wished she wouldn't be so darn rambunctious.

I opened my eyes again to see her chewing on her lower lip and looking like she'd been caught swiping eggs at somebody else's hen house. "I'm okay," I said calm and easy like. "Why don't you drag a chair over here so we can talk?"

Eban coughed. He'd walked to the back corner of the kitchen. "Lacey, while you're at it, will you throw the latch down for me after I go?" he asked.

She turned toward him. "Of course, Eban, are you leaving?"

"I've got a few chores to do yet. I'll see you two at supper." He opened the door.

I knew I didn't want to go the cabin for supper. I wasn't up to facing Maggie right now. And besides, Lacey was with me. "I'm going to stay here, Eban. Smooth things over for me will you?" I said it softly so to not jar my head.

He took a quick glance at Lacey and grinned. "I'll take care of it, son," he said.

But she looked back to me, her blue eyes locked into mine. "Oh no! You need your supper," she said, sounding like a mother duck now. "I'll cook something for you. I owe you that anyway." She glanced over at Eban. "Will you apologize for me too?"

He gave her a nod. "Sure! And Tom, you get as much rest as you can," he ordered.

I closed my eyes and began to breathe deep and slow again. The door slammed shut and the latch clicked down. I heard her walk to the table and rustle around a bit. Next a scraping sound came from dragging a chair across the floor.

It creaked as she sat. "This is my fault," she said softly but with a tiny shiver in her tone. "If I hadn't come here you wouldn't be hurt. I'm so sorry."

It seemed like she wanted to cry and right now that seemed more frightful than getting shot. "No! It's not your fault, Lacey. I just fell, that's all." There, I did it again. Once you start lying you can't stop. That's what Pa had told me. Pa was right.

"You got some new britches and shirts. They look nice," she

cooed.

"Thanks." She'd changed the subject on me. I was glad. Her voice sounded stronger and sweeter, a lot more like it usually did. She liked my new pants. That made me feel some better.

"You got a new hat, too," she went on. "A sombrero, I like it."

I couldn't put a finger on it but something in her tone sounded serious now, like she had a point to make. "Eban brought it. I like it too," I said.

"Did he bring you the shotgun at the same time?" she asked with a bite to her words.

Now I knew she had a point to make. I opened my eyes. She sat facing me near the edge of the cot. In her lap she held my blue army cap, a finger wiggling through the hole in the top. I gulped. "It tore when I fell," I knew she was on to me but I still had to keep to my story.

She turned the cap around and stuck a finger through another hole in the back where the ball came out. "Did it tear here when you fell too?" she went on, her voice soft again but her eyes rock hard.

I was tired of lying and Lacey knew anyway. I decided to come clean but I still couldn't tell her everything. "It was Jeremiah Wiggins. He shot at me outside town," I admitted.

"Who's Jeremiah Wiggins and why would he shoot at you?" she wailed. "You're the sweetest person I know."

It was hard for me to believe she didn't know Jeremiah. "Don't you remember? Him and his brother Jed were the first two customers you met the day you got here. He says you're his girl. He claims you, and wants me to leave you alone."

"No!" she yelled. Her face wrinkled, the corners of her mouth sagged. "It's my fault. I knew it. It's my fault." She was blubbering now. She hopped out of the chair, flopped onto the cot beside me and buried her head across my chest. "I'm sorry. I'm so sorry," she whimpered. The words came out splattered with deep sighs and sobs. Her tears fell like winter rain.

I'd never even talked much to a girl like I'd done with Lacey, and now she bawled so hard my new shirt already soaked through. I didn't want her to cry, but I didn't know what to do about it so I put my hand on her shoulder. That brought the throbbing back to my head but I gritted my teeth and tried to bear it like a man.

"Come on, Lacey. It ain't your fault. Jeremiah's been

drinking too much. He ain't right in the head, Eban says." I patted her shoulder, and felt awful awkward doing it.

"No! It is my fault. I flirted with everybody that day, hoping my Papa would hear where I am. Now people are trying to kill you because of me. Oh, I'm so stupid," she said, her words still broken by her sniffles.

It seemed that the harder Lacey cried the more my head hurt. I liked the way she laid across me on the cot, I liked it a lot, but it would be so much better if the pounding stopped. "Lacey, stop crying!" I moaned. "My head's killing me." Before I'd thought it over I'd said it. It simply slipped out of my mouth.

"Oh no!" Her head popped up and she looked at me. Tears streaked down her cheeks from red, puffy eyes, her mouth twisted into a serious frown. "I'm such a mess," she said. "Somebody's trying to shoot you and all I can do is blubber like baby Josie."

But as soon as she pulled away and I couldn't feel her across me anymore, I kicked myself for what I'd said. More than anything—more than my aching head, or the possibility that Jeremiah Wiggins would take another shot at me or whatever evil skullduggery Reid Harrison, Frank Barney and the man in the red shirt might cook up—I wanted Lacey's warm body back against mine. I reached up with my left hand, and with one hand now on each shoulder, gently pulled her to me.

As my eyes locked into hers the crying stopped. I breathed fast, like a colt after a sprint. Her flowery scent excited me like it had that first day. I closed my eyes and our lips met. Her mouth opened. My tongue found hers. A new throbbing in my roll-up pants pushed my pounding head from my thoughts. My arms wrapped around her body and I pulled her into me tight as I dared—and then tighter still.

"Oh, Tom—yes," she whispered, breathless.

5

The sun had barely nosed over the Sierra when I rode by the Round Tent Saloon. I couldn't help a rash of goose bumps, fearing maybe Jeremiah would pop from the flap like yesterday. But no one was out and drinking yet. The saloon didn't even open till near noon.

I rode Maggie's chestnut, Rojo, a copper colored stallion with a mane and tail a tad darker than his coat. Way faster than the dun the chestnut would come in handy if I got in a tight spot. Maggie almost never took him out anymore so Rojo pranced and danced, ready to run and clearly happy to be out of the stable.

Obadiah, the old stableman, had helped me get a scabbard for the shotgun tied under the left saddle skirt, and I'd tucked Maggie's little gun into the waistband of my new brown roll up pants so I could get to it easy. Wearing my green work shirt and the wide brimmed straw Mexican sombrero pulled down low on my forehead, even folks who knew me hadn't recognized me when I rode by. Maybe Eban had been right, maybe Jeremiah Wiggins would mistake me for a Mexican fellow and that might give me the time I needed to slip up on him. And that's just what I calculated to do because I'd set my mind on getting to exactly why Jeremiah shot me, and to make darn sure it didn't happen again—no matter what that took.

All night long, after Lacey had gone to the cabin, I'd tossed and turned, thinking about it all, worrying, fretting. Would I shoot Jeremiah Wiggins if push came to shove? I never did come up with any feel-good-about-it answer. There was nothing to feel good about. Lord knows I didn't want to shoot anybody, but when it came to shoot or be shot I'd be shooting. My mind set on it, I had no ground to give. I didn't intend to chicken out.

Yesterday, right after Eban told me Maggie would be working at the cafe again, I figured I'd do this today. I didn't let on what I planned, not to Eban or Lacey. Nobody was going to talk me out of it and sure as the sun comes up every morning one of them would be telling me no—no doubt about it. Then I could only sit around and wait for Jeremiah to show up and shoot me in the back. Better I face this on my own terms. The idea of somebody out to kill me sent frightful chills through my very bones. They shot at me yesterday. Today I was lucky to be alive.

At the Coloma Road I kept going straight along a horse path out of town. Men used this trail a lot less than Main Street. It still followed the creek but mostly only miners came this far. Some worked out in the stream washing dirt in low sided, wide pans, trying to separate the heavier gold from the soil. A miner who hit on a big pocket could wash out a lot of ore in a very short time. Hangtown Creek was loaded with gold. That's why so many men came here to mine.

I gave Rojo his head and he sped up to a trot. A gully started a little way down the stream and ran on for a while. Doak Wiggins, Jeremiah's pa, worked a little ways after it leveled out. But here only scrub brush and grass grew between the trail and the stream, yet to the south pine trees crowded the road.

The wind in my face whipped up the fire in my soul and forced my thoughts far from the normal day-to-day plodding of a team of mules pulling a heavy wagon. The sweet smell of pine, the gentle babble of the creek and the harsh shriek of a hawk jumbled together with the steady clatter of iron shoes on hard clay and gave me a feeling of unfettered freedom. I nudged the chestnut's flank and Rojo answered with a full gallop. The speed felt wonderful, powerful and so natural. For a while I almost forgot where I headed—and why. Then the creek dropped off into the gully on my right and ahead the trail made a sharp bend to the south. I pulled on the reins and slowed Rojo to a trot before the turn.

The road now ran up against the side of the gulch and I could look down to the stream below. No one mined here so this was one of the loneliest places along the creek. I rounded the curve and saw a rider coming on an old, plodding plow horse. A man stepped from the woods directly behind him. He wore a red shirt. He raised a rifle, aimed right this way. This was the second day in a row somebody pointed a gun at me.

The rifle smoked. I heard the shot. Trembling, I yanked Rojo's reins hard to turn him. The horse sensed my fear and sped back toward town. Beyond the curve I pulled off into the pines and yanked the shotgun from the scabbard, hopped to the ground and tied Rojo to a limb. I cowered behind a large pine near the trail and cocked one hammer of the scattergun.

Quickly I checked myself but saw no sign I'd been hit. A small comfort, but this getting shot at had to stop. I couldn't be lucky every day. I heard a horse coming fast. I pulled the shotgun to my shoulder and took a deep breath.

A pinto, with Red Shirt franticly slapping his rump, galloped full bore around the turn. The guy didn't even look in my direction. He rode by like a bolt from the blue, dead set to get away I reckoned. I didn't have time to even ponder pulling the trigger. After all, I hadn't come for Red Shirt. Still, I thought in hindsight, maybe I should've shot him.

Carefully I crept closer to the edge of the trail and peeked toward town. There I saw Red Shirt, still going at a full gallop, splash across Hangtown Creek and head up the hill on the Coloma Road. I watched till long after the pinto disappeared into the trees, fearful that he would double back. Finally it dawned on me that maybe he didn't even know it had been me back there. After all I had on the Mexican sombrero and like it might throw Jeremiah off my scent, it could do the same to the guy in the red shirt. And all lined up in row like we were he could've been aiming at the guy on the plow horse instead of me.

Somehow, in all the excitement, I forgot about the fellow riding the nag, but now I reflected he hadn't come by here. That puzzled me. Could it be that Red Shirt really did shoot at him? It didn't make sense right off, but it sure seemed somebody got shot.

Not wanting to ponder too long, I hopped on Rojo and hurried back around the curve. The plow horse stood by the gully. I grabbed the nag's reins and looked over the edge. A man lay face down at the bottom, fancy boots half in the water, a red patch spread across the seat of his pants. It had to be Jeremiah Wiggins. Red Shirt shot him for sure. But I couldn't get my mind around why? Still, I'd been shot and now Jeremiah had too, and all after I went looking for Lacey's pa.

I didn't know if he'd bought the farm or not but figured I had to find out. However the sides of the gully looked way too steep for a horse. I turned Rojo and led the old nag back toward town till I found a spot easy enough to ride down. I splashed through the creek back to Jeremiah.

I thought about pulling out the shotgun again but somehow he didn't seem much of a threat. Still he could be playing possum so

I grabbed Maggie's little gun just in case. A lot of blood soaked Jeremiah's shirt along his shoulder and back from a hole just beside the shoulder blade. I wished Eban was here. He always knew what to do in a spot like this and I sure didn't. But I had to do something, so with the little gun in hand I knelt and gave Jeremiah a shake. He didn't make a sound.

Figuring Jeremiah didn't have much fight left in him I put the pistol in my pocket. And because blood bubbled out of the hole in his back he likely still lived but must be hurt pretty bad. Eban cleaned my head wound with whiskey. I reckoned I should do the same for Jeremiah before I put on a bandage to plug up the wound, but I didn't have any whiskey. I never touched the stuff and after it destroyed my Pa I swore I never would. But Jeremiah reeked of it even this early in the morning. Maybe he had some.

Inside the first saddlebag I opened, right on top of everything, I found a half empty bottle and grinned, remembering how Memphis, a gambler who'd helped me out in Coloma last year, always said that a man who drank too much had his fill of Old Buzzard's Breath, and Jeremiah sure had rotten smelling breath. I never saw Memphis take a drink. A man who gambles drunk always loses, Memphis said. Now it seemed like Jeremiah had gambled drunk—and lost. I reached back in the saddlebag and pulled out a worn shirt. It would do for a bandage.

I cut away the clothes over the wound and poured a splash of whiskey on it. That brought a weak, whiney moan, but blood still pumped out pretty fast. I took a piece of the shirt I'd just cut off and folded it over a few times, put it over the hole and pressed down. After a while the bleeding stopped. I tore the shirt into strips and managed to get a bandage tied around Jeremiah.

Now I had to get him onto the plow horse, and since he was heavier than me that could be tricky. It would help if I could wake him. I rolled him onto his back. He looked a mess with two black eyes, red welts on both cheeks, and his lips scabbed over bad. He had more bruises than he should have from me only pelting him one time in the snoot. I swabbed his face with a whiskey soaked cloth. He groaned and his eyes fluttered open.

At first he stared directly ahead, an empty look about him. I figured maybe he was still rattled but decided more likely he'd be scared. After all, he hadn't seen the guy in the red shirt. He'd had only seen a fellow in a straw sombrero and now that guy gawked back at him. Jeremiah might figure I'm the one who shot him.

So I put on a comforting smile. "Take it easy," I said. "I'm going to get you out of here and up to Maggie's place. She'll fix you up."

It looked like a whole bucket of doubt washed across his face. "Why?" he whispered, his voice awful weak.

I didn't know if Jeremiah asked why I shot him or why I helped him. There was only one way to find out. "Do you know the guy in the red shirt? He shot you in the back," I told him as honestly as I could.

Surprise crept into Jeremiah's eyes. "K.O.—no—friend," he mumbled in weak, breathy, broken words, and it seemed to me that a little talk took a lot of trying.

"If I help you do you think you can get on your horse?" I asked, wondering if Jeremiah would give up the ghost right here and now. He sounded so pitiful and looked half dead already.

But he gave a feeble nod and whispered, "Try."

I pulled him up to where he sat without my help, brought the plow horse over so he could reach the stirrup and helped him get to his feet. Jeremiah gritted his teeth hard but didn't whine. He had sand in his craw. I'll give him that. We got his left foot stuck into the stirrup and I heaved him up by his other boot. He flopped into the saddle with a bothersome groan.

All that effort gave me an up-close, personal look at his footwear. It sure seemed peculiar for a man to have on pants that were patched in the rear, and way shorter than mine when Lacey teased me over them, and still sport a pair of fancy, handmade Mexican riding boots with snakeskin all along the foot part and fancy carvings in well-tanned leather going up the leg. Jeremiah's high-toned footwear didn't match his homemade pants at all.

But I didn't have time for pondering boots and britches. Jeremiah needed the shoulder tended right away. "You all right?" I asked to make sure.

His face twisted with pain but he managed a small nod. I grabbed the nag's reins, climbed on Rojo and rode slowly upstream toward town. I glanced back a lot to make sure he didn't tumble off, certain that when we got to the cabin I'd have the dickens to pay from Maggie and Lacey both.

##

I'd raced down the cabin steps two at a time and jumped up on Rojo ready to ride when Lacey burst out the cabin door.

"Tom Marsh, you stop right where you are!" she yelled as she tore over to the split log rail and leaned out so far I thought she'd topple over.

I stopped. I'd almost made it out of here without telling anybody the whole story. Maggie had been busy looking Jeremiah over and getting him settled and stuff, and with Lacey helping her I'd figured to get out while the getting was good. "I've got to go," I said, trying my best to duck her questions.

"Did you shoot that boy, Tom?" A deep worry crossed her face.

"No, another fellow did. Does your Pa know a guy who wears a red shirt and a white straw hat with a blue bandana tied around his neck?" I asked, both to get her mind off me and maybe learn something at the same time.

I could tell she thought hard. "No, I don't remember a man like that, but I don't know everybody Papa knows," she finally said. "Is he the one that shot him?"

"Yeah, I thought at first he wanted to shoot me. It scared me near to death."

"Is this about my Papa?" Now she looked really upset.

I shrugged. "I'm really not sure, Lacey," I said, hoping she'd let it go.

Her hands went to her mouth. "Oh, Tom, this is my fault. I got you involved."

I knew I had to say something fast to make her feel better. "No! It ain't your fault," I fired back. "There's swindlers and scalawags out there who stoop to shooting folks. If your Pa ain't tied up with them, he must be against them. I guess that puts him on the right side. You ought to be proud of him for that."

A tiny smile bloomed on her red lips. "My Papa would be on the right side of every swindler and scalawag. That's for sure." She stuck her chin out, proud of her Papa.

Her smile cheered me. At least she wouldn't cry now. "Maggie ain't going to be able to make it to the cafe today, what with taking care of Jeremiah and little Josie both," I said. "I guess that leaves it up to us. I want to find Jeremiah's pa and let him know what happened. I'll be back after that. We might have to open the cafe late."

"No, I can get things started. I'm a pretty good cook too you know." She glanced at the cabin door. "If you wait for me to tell Maggie I'll ride down the hill with you."

Now I smiled wide. "Don't take too long," I said. I liked her a lot when she helped out, and she'd already been a real big help at the cafe and with Josie. Rojo snorted and pawed the ground, ready to ride, but I held him steady and waited for her. In no time the front door slammed shut and she bounced down the steps and crawled up on the nag.

"Let's go," she yelled and rode off down the hill in front of me.

It seemed like she looked forward to working at the cafe by herself. That would mean she'd cook lunch for today. If it was half as good as the supper she made for me last night folks would be mighty pleased with it, for a fact. I followed her across the log bridge and down the street to the front of the cafe.

"Keep the doors latched till I get back." I warned. "I hate to think of you here all by yourself with lonely miners everywhere about."

She handed me the reins to the nag, then leaned over from the plow horse and kissed my cheek. "I'll be fine," she vowed. "You're the one that needs worrying over. Hurry back, okay?"

"Soon as I can," I promised. It made me feel special when she kissed me like that and put me in a powerful hurry to get back to her, but I still waited till she was inside and I heard the latch go down before I rode off. I knew that if the wrong man knew her pa was Webster Lawson she could be in for a peck of trouble. That sat hard on my mind.

Town bustled with more miners than it had earlier and some Eastern guys already loafed outside the Round Tent. I nudged Rojo to a trot in case Red Shirt had doubled back and hid out inside the saloon. Past the Coloma Road I kicked Rojo up to a lope, about as fast as I thought I could push the old plow horse. We had a ways to go yet. I slowed up a little at the curve but sped up again on the other side.

At last the gully started to level out and six men worked hard at washing ore down a long wooden sluice with cleats along the bottom to catch the gold. They were dressed strange, with cone shaped hats, baggy clothes and shoes that looked like nothing more than a flat piece of leather held on by straps. Each one had a long ponytail hanging down his back. I heard Chinese mined around here but I'd never seen any till today. Now I had to find Doak Wiggins.

The first American looking fellow I asked shook his head and went back to panning ore, but the next one jerked a thumb downstream. I rode on. Pretty soon I saw Jed Wiggins standing ankle deep in the creek and sifting through a gold pan with his fingers, picking out nuggets from the gravel. Jed had the same dark hair and leathery, outdoor look about him as his brother. Yet I couldn't help notice how he didn't wear fancy boots like Jeremiah did, but his pants seemed about as raggedy.

He looked up as I neared. "Who are you?" he groused. "What are you doing with our horse?"

"It's Tom Marsh, Jed, and I'm bringing your horse back to you." I answered. Jed hadn't recognized me in the sombrero either.

"Jeremiah rode that horse this morning. What happened to him?"

"Somebody shot him, up by the gulch."

"You shot him. He said you was planning on killing him 'cause of that girl."

"I found him in the creek and took him to Maggie. She's fixing him up right now. Some guy in a red shirt shot him," I snorted. Taking blame for something I didn't do really rubbed me wrong.

"You're lying," Jed fired back.

That got my dander up. Jed didn't believe a word I said. I needed to turn his head around quick if I was going to get back to Lacey and the cafe in time for the noon crowd. "Come on, Jed. Think about it some." I snapped. "Would I take Jeremiah up to the place I live so that maybe Maggie can save his life, then bother to come back here with his horse if I shot him?" My anger came across clear and with it the certainty that what I said was the gospel truth.

Jed shrugged and hollered downstream. "Pa! Get up here. Jeremiah's been shot." He turned back to me. "Reckon you might have a point. We'll see what Pa has to say."

Right now I didn't give a tinker's dam what Doak Wiggins had to say and I wasn't of a mind to hang around and discuss things. "I got work to do," I growled. "I ain't got time for chit-chat," so I dropped the reins to the plow horse. "Your brother will be at Maggie's cabin, if he's still alive. I don't know who he got mixed up with, but it don't look like they was the best folks in town. I'll be at the cafe if you or your Pa wants me." I turned and rode hard back along the creek to town.

##

After dropping off Rojo at the stable I walked toward the cafe and kept stewing over something Jeremiah had said back in the gully. I hadn't had much time for jawing over things then, but now I wished I'd asked exactly what he'd meant after I told him that Red Shirt had done the shooting and he'd mumbled 'K.O.—no—friend,' all busted up and whispery. Likely Red Shirt went by the name of K.O. and knowing his name seemed pretty darn important, but after that things got muddled. Did Jeremiah mean he didn't believe K.O. shot him because K.O. was his friend, or did he mean that K.O. wasn't his friend?

In the long run K.O. did the shooting so he wasn't a friend, but how Jeremiah knew him might turn out pretty meaningful to what had happened so far. Maybe it could give me a look see into why Webster Lawson came to the gold country in the first place, though I still couldn't be sure of any connection between K.O. and Jeremiah, the mining cooperative and that whole gang of riffraff and Lacey's pa. Talk about things getting all mucked up. Still, my gut told me I followed the right trail. It was a lot like a hornet's nest, if you stir it up you're liable to get stung, and I got stung bad yesterday.

Maybe, if Maggie can pull Jeremiah through this, he'll be willing to talk. She couldn't say anything about his chances earlier, at least not until she'd had a better look, and there ain't no way to be sure, but Maggie had a gift. Folks showed up at the cabin with busted arms and legs that needed setting, or deep cuts that needed stitching, and Maggie always helped them. Men everywhere around here knew about her. The miners along Hangtown Creek thought the world of her. Still, a gunshot ain't much like a busted bone, but she saved Eban's life when Scarface shot him in the chest and I felt dang sure she could save Jeremiah too.

Figuring Lacey would be in the cafe's kitchen I walked around to the back door and knocked. I didn't have to wait long before I heard her footsteps. The door opened and she stood there with a big smile on her face, wearing the blue and white apron dusted with flour. When I stepped inside she threw her arms around my neck and kissed me hard. I couldn't help myself. I hugged her tight and thought about carrying her to the cot in the corner.

She pulled away with a sparkle in her eyes and said, "Take it easy, big fellow. I've got lunch in the oven." Before I caught my breath she headed back to the table where six pie pans with the crust already in sat beside a bowl of dried apples soaking.

"Apple pie, that's one of my favorites," I said. "What's in the oven?"

"Four chickens and four loaves of bread, and I've got peas and carrots and a bunch of potatoes boiling on the top."

I grinned, "Smells great, I'm hungry already."

She poured a cup of sugar into the apple slices and stirred everything around with a big spoon. "This is for the customers, you and me got work to do," she pointed out.

"Yes ma'am," I said and I gave her a small bow. "I'll sweep up the dining room, if you don't mind."

She giggled and kissed me again, quick and on the cheek. "I'm glad you got back all in one piece."

"Yeah, me too," I said with a smile. I sure did like it when she seemed to care about me like this. I liked it so much that I didn't want to leave any more, even to go into the next room, so I started to shuffle my feet around while I thought of something to say. "Ah, well, uh—"

"Get on with you," she snapped. "Folks will want their lunch anytime now." She waved the spoon in my face to shoo me away but grinned from ear to ear as she did.

In the dining room I wiped the tables with a rag then swept the floor with a good, stiff broom. While I straightened out the chairs under a table next to one of the windows, I saw Doak and Jed Wiggins pass by on their way to the cabin. Doak rode a nice looking sorrel mare that reminded me a lot of Sadie, the horse I'd ridden when I came to the gold country, but Jed was plodding along on the old plow horse. At the rate the nag could go, Doak and Jed must have left right after I did. Maybe they'd be back here after they had a chance to see Jeremiah.

I unlatched the front door and walked over to the wall between the dining room and the kitchen and swung open the shutters over the plank counter. When Maggie worked by herself the men would walk up to the opening and say hello, then she would fill up a plate and set it on the ledge. Maggie knew most everybody who came in anyway so it worked real good for her. I'd closed it, but with Lacey cooking today I knew the miners would give me no end of grief if they couldn't see her.

Lacey had pulled the bread out of the oven, and it smelled great. The apple pies were nowhere in sight so they must be baking now. A large bowl of mashed potatoes sat on the table and Lacey stood by the stove, stirring a skillet full of giblet gravy. She was whipping up a lunch the miners weren't apt to forget anytime soon. But somehow, deep down, I knew I was the one Lacey wanted to impress with her good cooking. She hummed a bright tune while she worked, a lot like Maggie always did, and seemed completely happy and right at home in the cafe's kitchen.

She noticed me through the opening and smiled. "Can you get some water from the well, Tom? I need to start coffee."

"Right away," I grinned back at her and took a quick look around the dining room. Satisfied I'd done a good job I went into the kitchen. Near the washstand I picked up the two oak buckets and slid out the back door. While walking to the well I could see the mane and tail of the sorrel, almost white against her brown coat, as she stood beside Maggie's porch. Doak Wiggins was up there looking in on Jeremiah.

After I filled the two buckets I lugged them toward the kitchen and thought how I'd give a pair of my new pants to see what was going on up at the cabin. Would Jeremiah be okay? Would he tell his Pa anything about what he'd done to get those fancy boots? I felt like a meddling old school marm, but couldn't help myself. I had a lot riding on Jeremiah. If Maggie could save him he might be willing to explain some things that I'd pondered on real hard, and without getting much for all my brooding.

Back in the kitchen I gave one bucket to Lacey, poured the other into a wash pan and set it on the stove to warm, then set about scraping out the pots and pans Lacey had used to cook with. When the wash water heated up enough I hauled it to the washstand and started to scour out everything that I'd scraped. I always wanted to get a head start on the hardest work, and scrubbing the cooking gear topped the list.

I'd finished drying the last of the heavy, black iron pots when the bell over the door rang, and through the open shutters I saw Morton shuffling toward the counter. Oh Lord, I thought, he must've heard from somebody that Maggie would be here today, and that somebody was likely Eban. After all the grumbling he did Friday because she wasn't here he'd probably bellyache a hundred times worse if he thought he'd been lied to.

I rushed over to cope with any storm that might blow in but Morton made it to the opening first. I pulled on my Sunday smile. "Good to see you, Mr. Morton," I said.

He slowly rolled his tired, bloodshot eyes around the kitchen. "Where's Maggie? She's supposed to be here," he carped in his usual gruff way.

I tried hard to keep my smile up and speak nice and easy. "Maggie had a fellow show up hurt this morning so she's back at the cabin helping him out." Morton's sour expression didn't change. I took that as a good sign.

"I saw Doak Wiggins' mare tied out in front. Doak hurt?" he snarled.

"No, it's his son, Jeremiah." Morton was one of the biggest gossipmongers in town. I figured he might've come in to find out who Maggie patched up.

Morton gave a small nod, not a shake like most do when they hear somebody's been hurt. "That boy's rotten to the core. Probably deserved what he got. I feel bad for old Doak though. He's a good man. Don't figure, him having such a no good offspring. What happened to that fool boy anyhow?"

"Somebody shot him."

"I ain't surprised, like to have shot him myself down at the Round Tent Saturday. He kept badgering me about joining that dang mining cooperative, like he thought I might. I got a good claim going. Why on earth would I share it with a bunch of city folk fresh off the boat?"

Morton naturally had a nasty way but I was glad he was yelling about Jeremiah and not Maggie. And what he said sounded pretty darn interesting.

He flipped a gruff backhand into the air and kept at it. "Crooks! They ain't nothing but crooks, that whole mining cooperative. Three men got killed in Coloma. Two Mexican fellers was shot in their sleep. An old man was beat to death. They all had good-paying claims going. Now that dang mining cooperative's working them claims. Every day somebody's talking about miners from Chile, Mexico, even them Chinamen, getting run off a good placer deposit. It ain't right I tell you. It just ain't right."

"So what does Jeremiah care if you or anybody else joins the mining cooperative?" I said, trying to sound like a guy making small talk, not wanting Morton to know I had such a big interest. He'd blab it all over town.

"How do I know what Jeremiah Wiggins gets if he wrestles some fool into joining them hornswogglers?" he grumbled. "He's got enough money to drink highfaluting French champagne and wear them fancy hand-tooled boots. He don't get that from Doak Wiggins, you can bet on it." Morton's voice grew loud and full of heat.

A steaming hot plate slid onto the counter and I realized Lacey stood right beside me. "Here's your lunch, sir," she said in her sweet, honey-flavored voice.

Morton looked down, sniffed at the mouthwatering blend of smells that sat practically under his whiffer and quickly picked up the plate. "Why this looks right tasty," he said as obligingly as I'd ever heard him talk. He gaped at Lacey with what was as near to a smile as the old codger could conjure up on such a wrinkled, sour face. "Thank you, miss. Thank you much," he mumbled before he gobbled up a healthy dollop of potatoes and gravy, nodded his approval, hurried to the nearest table and began muscling food into his mouth like a starving wolf would a deer.

I stared at him in wonder until Lacey bumped me with her hip and jarred me back to the here and now. She grinned like a miner who'd found a five-pound nugget. Then she winked, spun around, and sashayed off. What a gal I thought as my eyes followed the swaying blue flowers on her backside all the way to the stove.

But the bell on the door jingled and five men walked in. Things got awful busy in the cafe real quick and I didn't have much time to mull over Jeremiah except for a small break here and there and each time, in my mind, I would see K.O. pull the trigger at Jeremiah's back. But more men would walk in and I'd hustle from table to table again, toting in plates full of food and hauling empty ones back to the kitchen to wash.

Finally the bell dinged as the last of the noon crowd left. I wiped the sweat from my face and started to straighten the tables. Taking advantage of the breather my mind wandered back to Jeremiah Wiggins and whether or not Maggie could pull him through. With Doak's mare still at the cabin maybe Jeremiah lived.

Out of the corner of my eye I saw Lacey framed in the

counter opening. "Two plates for table three," she called like she'd done all day. I walked over, picked up the food and carried it to a table by a window, set the plates down and went back to tiding up, my mind all tangled up by the shooting.

"Aren't you hungry?" I heard her ask from behind me.

I spun. She sat at the table where I'd put the food. "Oh! That's for us. I guess wasn't thinking," I said and sat down across from her. "I'm starved. This looks great."

She beamed at the compliment. "I was afraid I'd lost you. All morning you've been in a daze. Is it about that boy who got shot?" she asked.

"Yeah, I guess so. It's all real strange, not what I expected to happen. I'm not sure about a lot of things now." I shrugged.

"This has to do with my Papa too, doesn't it?" she moaned. "That's why somebody shot at you. You're trying to find Papa and somebody wants to kill you for it. Oh Lord! If something happens to you I'll just die." Her face twisted up like it did before she cried.

I didn't want that. I'd had enough trouble for one day. "No! Nothing's your fault," I snapped at her and regretted it as soon as I did. Her eyes clouded up and a tear rolled down her cheek. "I'm sorry," I said a lot softer. "I don't mean to yell. I just don't want you to worry. Yeah, I've been looking for your Pa and I think that's what all this trouble is about. But I'll grant you I'm confused. Maybe you can help me some."

She dabbed at her eyes with a napkin and when she pulled it away she wore a small smile. "I'll do anything to find Papa. I hope you know that."

"Well, for now just let me ask you a few things. Do you remember when you first showed up here?" She nodded so I went on, "There was that guy you almost ran into at the door. You took a swing at him with your purse."

"Yeah!" she blurted. "He's a dirty lecher. He put his hand on my . . ." She looked real sheepish and giggled. "You know where he put it," she added.

I grinned along with her. "Yeah, maybe I do. His name is Reid Harrison. Have you ever met him before? Did your Papa know him?"

She puckered her lips, thinking hard. "I don't believe so, but it's like the guy you asked me about this morning, Papa knows a lot of people. I wish I could help."

I shrugged and started in on the food but it wasn't long before I told her the whole story, from talking to Reid Harrison on Sunday to watching Jeremiah get shot this morning. I threw in every detail I could think of, what each guy looked like, what kind of horse K.O. rode, the fancy Mexican boots, but so far nothing rang a bell with her. She'd listened hard, soaking up every word I said, her forehead knotted, her face serious, like she was trying hard to figure something out.

I really didn't want to interrupt her pondering but I still had to keep my manners in mind. "I'm getting some pie. Can I bring you a slice?"

She looked up and nodded and went right back to puzzling over things. I felt better as I walked into the kitchen because she didn't seem to be put out too much. I cut two wedges, popped each onto a plate and headed back to Lacey.

When I got to the dining room she blurted out to me, "There was something, a long time ago, during the war—"

"Yeah, tell me," I interrupted. I slid her pie across the table and hopped into my chair.

Her eyes found mine, a determined look on her face. "I don't know if this is anything but I remember it because of a Mexican guy named Santa Ana, his name always reminded me of Santa Claus and it happened right around Christmas time. My Papa told me about some American soldiers who came all the way from the east and were heading to San Diego, but the Mexicans chased them up a hill and all they had to eat was mule meat. Then some other Americans from San Diego showed up and ran the Mexicans away."

I cut her off. "Joshua and Eban were there. First they fought at a place called San Pasqual. The next day the Mexicans jumped them and chased them up the hill. They called it Mule Hill."

She gulped. "Yeah, that's the place. A man named Kit Carson snuck off and brought help. Everybody talked about Kit Carson in San Francisco. He was a big hero."

I nodded. "That's what happened, but what has this all got to do those varmints at the mining cooperative and Santa Ana? He's the Mexican President you know."

"Well, I'm not too sure. Papa said there was a guy called K.O. Manuel, I think, who went around the cantinas fist fighting for money, and he knew this guy Santa Ana. He got together with two men in San Diego that worked with Papa somehow who told him that the Americans were coming. Then K.O. told Santa Ana who sent some of his soldiers to stop our soldiers. When our soldiers got away Santa Ana said he would kill this K.O. guy and his two cronies if he caught them. Papa was real mad too. He called them all traitors and said they should face a firing squad. If these are the same guys, they're in trouble with everybody."

"Holy Moses!" I yelled, my apple pie untouched. "I'd bet anything that your Papa heard they were in the gold country and came here looking for them. But what happened to him?"

"I don't know," she whispered, a quiver in her voice.

"Now don't worry," I said, trying to sound sure of myself. "I've got some ideas. Maybe, if Eban will help me, I can find your Pa." Truthfully I had no ideas, at least nothing I could sink my teeth into, but I didn't want her bawling again so I'd lied. What did it matter anyway? I'd become an old hand at lying by now.

But she still smiled at me, not real bright but enough to make me think she felt okay about all this. And through the open window I caught a glimpse of the sorrel mare out in front. I turned for a better look. It was Doak Wiggins all right, with Jeremiah hanging on the back—alive.

While I lit the last lamp in the dining room I heard the rumble of a freight wagon coming this way. Eban should've been home long ago. He'd said he would look into things in Coloma so maybe he'd heard something to add to the story that Lacey recalled this afternoon. I walked out the front door.

Eban waved. "Fix me a plate. I'll be right back," he yelled.

"Sure thing." I watched until the mules turned to the stable, went back inside and walked to the counter.

Lacey looked up from the kitchen table. She had two plates full of hot food ready to go. "Are you hungry?" she asked even though she had to know I was. She'd been real quiet and edgy all afternoon, ever since our talk about K.O. Manuel and his cronies.

"I'm starved," I said. "Eban will be here soon. We need to fix him some supper too."

She carried the two meals to the counter and set them down. "I'll get another one for him. You go ahead and eat," she said without a trace of sparkle in her voice.

"I'm glad he's coming. He's real late. Maybe he found something out in Coloma. But whether he did or not we need to talk," I muttered and picked up the food.

"Do you think he knows something about my Papa?" she asked.

Her face looked tired and tense. The fear I'd seen the first day we met haunted her eyes again. I knew Eban could easily have bad news about her Pa. She had every right to be afraid. "Don't worry," I said matter of fact like. "Eban sounded excited and not stewing over bad news."

The corners of her mouth edged up a bit, sunnier but heedful. I hoped, for both our sakes, that Eban did have good news. I put the plates on the table and sat, lost in thought about his mood when he'd waved. He did seem eager to get back here and that bode well for good news. All things considered, I just wanted Lacey to be happy. For some reason, when she smiled, it always made me feel on top of the world.

She came in from the kitchen with Eban's supper and three cups of hot coffee and sat. She kept her head down and didn't look up at all. It wasn't like her to be so bashful.

"Are you okay?" I asked.

"I'm fine," she said, but her head stayed low and her voice sounded glum.

"I don't believe you," I shot back. "Look at me."

"No, I'm fine, honest." A sniffle, followed by a sob, gave her away. She was crying again and as usual I'd been a total dunce about it.

I wanted to understand why she needed to bawl when things got thorny because it really didn't make much sense to me. I guess girls cried a lot but I don't remember Maggie ever turning on the waterfall at the drop of a hat like Lacey was apt to do. "Maybe Eban has some good news," I offered. "There ain't no reason to be crying till you know for sure." It sounded like sure-enough good advice to me.

"Oh, I'm sorry," she began. "I don't mean to be such a bother but I can't help it. I'm so worried about my Papa. I miss him a lot. I should've heard something about him by now, but it's like he's vanished into thin air." She dabbed at her eyes with a napkin. "I'll be okay," she added. "Just give me a little time."

It seemed like she wanted to buck up and face things so I dug into the potatoes and gravy and quickly took a bite of roast chicken. Lacey had done a great job today. Her cooking tasted out of this world. Almost all the miners who ate here said so. I knew that if her food could make Morton quit his bellyaching and eat it must be special.

The front door opened. The bell dinged. Eban strode in and pitched his straw hat onto a table. "Howdy folks. That chicken sure smells fine." He pulled out a chair and sat. "I talked to Wimmer at the saw mill," he went on. "Did you meet him when you were there, Lacey?" He looked into her face for the first time and then put his hand on her arm. "Oh my, do you want to tell old Eban about it, dear?" he said, sounding as gentle as I'd ever heard him.

She stirred her fork around the potatoes and shrugged. "I miss my Papa so much. I'm afraid something horrible happened to him," she said but didn't look up.

Eban smiled. "I don't blame you for missing your Pa, but I wouldn't write him off just yet. Let me tell you about my talk with Wimmer. He runs the saw mill, you know, and has a finger in most everything that happens around Coloma. Well, not long ago he got word that a government feller would be looking into some varmint that might be in town. Seems like it had to do with something from the war. If the feller needs help Wimmer is supposed to give it to him—anything he wants—and when the feller is done he'll come by and let Wimmer know. Well, I figure that feller is Webster Lawson and he ain't let Wimmer know he's done yet. Lacey, your Pa's still around."

Eban looked over at Lacey with a bright smile, sure he'd brought good news for her. She dabbed her eyes again and whispered, "Tell him, Tom."

"Wait up now," I pled. "What Eban said sounds like good news to me too."

"Maybe he's dead," she cried. "Maybe that's why Papa hasn't talked to Mr. Wimmer." She looked up, her eyes red, the tears in the corners covering her fear, magnifying it like a spyglass did for things far away.

"Hold on here!" Eban snarled. "Where's Maggie? She said she'd be working here today?" He turned my way. "What's going on? What are you supposed to tell me?"

I frowned. After Lacey told me about K.O. Manuel and Mule Hill, I thought we'd latched on to something important, something that would help find her Pa, but in no time flat all her worrying, fretting and crying put a bucket full of doubt in my mind. Now I wasn't sure about anything. Still, I knew I needed to tell Eban the whole story so I started at the beginning. "I went after Jeremiah this morning, Eban."

"Jeremiah!" he growled like I knew he would.

"Look Eban a lot happened today and, thanks to Lacey remembering some real important stuff, we have a good idea what's going on with her Pa. I ain't sure why she wants to whimper so much about it all 'cause I think we got a good chance of finding him and maybe pretty darn soon. So why don't we just have our supper and talk this over serious-like and see if we can come up with a plan?" I hoped to turn everybody's bad mood back into a good one.

Across the table Lacey stared at me with the same heedful smile she'd had earlier, but Eban suddenly beamed wide and nodded heartily. "That's a fine idea, Tom. Let's have supper and meantime you can explain your little visit to Jeremiah Wiggins. And Lacey, you ought to be right grateful that Tom cares about you enough to do what he's doing to find your Pa."

Her eyelashes fluttered fast and a hint of white teeth flashed between her lips. "You're right, Eban, he's pretty special," she said and a taste of sweetness crept back into her voice.

Eban started in on his mashed potatoes and gravy while I told him the story of my trip to the Wiggins place, K.O. shooting Jeremiah by the gully and me pulling the wounded Jeremiah from the stream and getting him to Maggie who patched him up. Next Lacey told about K.O. and how he'd told the Mexicans the stuff that led to the battles at San Pasqual and Mule Hill. Afterwards I jumped back in to tie everything together.

All the while Eban sat and ate but his face burned redder and redder till it shone brighter than the lamps. "That low down rotten sack of . . ." he finally fumed, but stopped short of saying something in front of Lacey he'd regret. "I'll be back in Coloma tomorrow. Then I'll dig out that stinking varmint and drub his back-shooting face into the ground."

I thought steam would shoot from Eban's ears, but I'd put all this together and got Sunday punched and shot at doing it. No way could anybody leave me out at the finish. "I'm going with you, Eban," I asserted with a large dollop of grit.

"No you ain't," he roared, pounding his fist onto the table.

"This is too dangerous for a boy. Maggie would skin me alive if anything happened to you."

I leaped to my feet, toppling my chair over as I did. "I'm going, Eban," I yelled. "You can't stop me. I'm the one that started looking for Lacey's Pa and I'll be the one to find him. I don't care what this K.O. character might do. And I ain't no boy!" My fists thumped down on the table, knuckles white against the bare wood tabletop.

"You don't understand," Eban yelled back, knocking his own chair over as he jumped up and faced me nose to nose. "This ain't no man we're after, it's the devil himself. I seen him once in San Francisco, back when they still called it Yerba Buena. He beat a Mexican feller within an inch of his life, would've killed him if folks hadn't pulled him off. He loved it. He wanted to kill him. He enjoyed it."

"I don't care," I bellowed. "I'm going and that's that!"

"Stop it! Both of you stop it!!" Lacey screamed and sprang to her feet. "I don't want anybody to go. I don't want either of you hurt." Then she kicked at her chair and it too clattered to the floor. "It's my fault. I never should have come here!" she wailed and rushed out through the front door, slamming it so hard it bounced right back open again.

I wanted to kick myself. It seemed the more I tried to help Lacey the more trouble I got into with her. Eban had a sheepish look across his face, like he felt the same way. But here we were, eyeball to eyeball, two great friends yelling at each other like cats in the barn. Plus I could hear Lacey sobbing her eyes out from in front of the cafe and I felt awful about it.

I yanked my chair off the floor and sat down, elbows on the table, face in my fists. Then I felt Eban's hand on my shoulder and looked up at him.

"I'm sorry I hollered at you, son," he said softly. "I shouldn't have. It's just that so many good men died at San Pasqual, and now this. It's something I thought was buried in the past," he added, his tone real easy, like he usually talked.

"Yeah, I'm sorry too," I mumbled, not able to understand why when I try so hard to do the right thing sometimes it turns out so wrong. I didn't understand at all.

Eban picked up his chair and sat. "Did you get a chance to talk to Jeremiah while you brought him to Maggie?"

"No, he was in rough shape and I worried more about him cashing his chips in, but I think there's a pile of stuff he could tell me, if he's willing."

"All right, how about you go down to the Wiggins place in the morning and see what you can pry out of him. After all, it sounds like you saved his life. I reckon he owes you. His Pa, Doak Wiggins, is a good man. He ain't going to let nothing bad happen to you at his house. You'll be safe there. Then you can catch up with me on the Coloma Road. We'll see if we can dig up Webster Lawson without stepping on any rattlesnakes. How does that sound?"

I gave him a wish-I-hadn't-done-it grimace. "That sounds great, Eban."

"That's good," he said. "Now I'd better go out and talk to Lacey. She's young and under a big strain for a girl her age. She's got a lot of spunk though. She'll be fine, but I'll walk her up to the cabin so you can get some sleep. Tomorrow might be a long day."

6

When Rojo and I rode out of the stable I saw her racing down the hill from the cabin, her yellow dress flapping as she ran.

"Tom, wait for me," she yelled.

I turned Rojo toward the bridge and leaped to the ground. She dashed across. I was glad to see her. After she ran out of the dining room last night, crying and yelling, I wasn't sure if she cared about me anymore. But straightaway I realized that she was coming fast and not about to stop. She bounced into me like an out-of-control boulder rolling downhill would run into a tree. I barely kept from toppling over.

She threw her arms around me. "Oh Tom, I couldn't let you go without seeing you," she whispered, her breath hot on my cheek.

"I'm glad you're here," I dropped Rojo's reins, wrapped my own arms around her and pulled her tight against my chest.

She kissed me full on the mouth and scrunched her body into mine. My breath came quick and so did that lump in my pants. I thought about the cot back at the cafe and how great it would be if we went there right now. But instead I put my hands on her shoulders and pushed her back. "I've got to go," I said softly.

She nodded, and I could see the sparkle of tears in her eyes but she wasn't blubbering or bawling like last night. "You come back to me, Tom Marsh. You hear?" Her lower lip twitched but her words had force. She meant what she said.

I kissed her again, then reached behind me and grabbed the reins. "Wait for me. I won't be long. I promise." I spun around, hopped on Rojo, gave him a kick and tore down the street. Just past the cafe I looked over my shoulder. She stood right where I'd left her, her eyes locked on me. I yanked off the sombrero and waved. She waved back, hopping up and down, her arm swinging wildly back and forth.

I let Rojo gallop all the way through town and didn't slow him until the trail turned. Here the gully sat too close to the road and seemed way too deep to chance taking the curve that fast. But I

hankered something awful to talk with Jeremiah Wiggins, maybe get some answers from him and make my way to Coloma as quick as I could. Today might be the biggest day of my life and my whole body tingled with excitement.

Maggie said that Jeremiah had been lucky. The gunshot hadn't hit anything important and she thought that bouncing down the side of the gully had done near as much damage to him as the wound. He'd lost a lot of blood though and that would keep him off his feed for a while. I sure hoped Jeremiah would be willing to talk about K.O. Manuel and his cohorts now that I'd saved his bacon.

The gully flattened out to my right and a new group of men stood around the same sluice box that I saw last time I passed, but these guys looked like fresh-off-the-boat easterners, not the Chinamen who'd been here before. Those men had been working hard, jabbering wildly at each other like folks do when they'd found gold. But the new guys mostly just drank. I thought back on Morton talking about how folks got run off good paying claims and wondered if that's what had happened to the Chinamen who'd worked here yesterday.

I'd find Doak Wiggins' place up ahead so I rode on. No one stood in the creek where I'd seen Jed yesterday but he'd yelled downstream for his Pa so I kept going till I saw the sorrel grazing on the far side of the water, a rough log shanty with a sod roof behind her. I turned Rojo and splashed across Hangtown Creek.

When I got close I stopped and yelled loud. "Hello, anybody home?"

"Keep your hands in front. I got a bead right down your gut." Whoever said it had a low, smooth voice that pleased the ear, though he still sounded old and ornery like Morton. But people pointing guns at me day in and day out sure got tiresome fast.

"Doak Wiggins?" I waited a bit but got no answer. "I'm Tom Marsh." I added. "I don't mean you no harm but I got to talk to Jeremiah. It's important."

"Jeremiah ain't of a mind to talk to you. Ride on." The deep voice boomed out from the west side of the shack.

"Maggie said Jeremiah would have bled to death real quick if I hadn't got to him when I did. I saved his life, Wiggins. Now he owes me. A lot more good people are in danger from the polecats Jeremiah worked with. How about it?"

"He tells me you was lying when you said some guy in a red

shirt did the shooting. He says you shot him 'cause of a girl you two fought over Sunday."

I had to get Doak Wiggins to understand things and pretty darn fast so I reckoned to tell him what I knew. "The man in the red shirt is called K.O. Manuel. Him, Reid Harrison and Frank Barney sold out Kearny's Army of the West to the Mexicans down south at San Pasqual and Mule Hill, and that got a lot of good men killed. Now they're up here bilking hardworking miners out of their claims and selling the fresh-off-the-boat guys a bill of goods. They've already killed three men in Coloma. There's an army man hunting for them. I'm out to find him. Things would go better for Jeremiah if he'd help me."

"You ain't no lawman. What can you do?" Doak barked.

"I'm looking for the army guy right now. I'll tell him what I found out and how Jeremiah helped. That ought to mean something."

"What makes you think Jeremiah knows anything about folks getting killed all the way over to Coloma? He told me he ain't even heard nothing about any of it."

It sounded like Doak Wiggins' deep voice had softened up some so I pushed him harder. "Maybe he don't, but why not let him tell me that?"

A big, black crow squawked from a tall pine across the creek, but Doak stayed quiet, hopefully mulling things over. At last he spoke, "You give your word you won't kill him?"

I rolled my eyes. I couldn't believe Doak thought I would come here to hurt Jeremiah after I'd saved his life yesterday. But I remembered how yesterday I'd planned on shooting Jeremiah if I had to. Maybe Doak had a point. "I swear. I only want to talk. You can listen in if you're worried," I said.

Doak didn't make me wait long. "Leave your horse where he is. Come in slow."

"You might help a lot of folks, Mr. Wiggins," I said and slid from Rojo careful so I wouldn't give Doak any excuse to shoot. I made sure to hold my hands in plain sight all the while I walked toward the shack. When I got a few feet away he stepped out wearing a beat up straw hat, a mud splattered plaid shirt and holding a battered flintlock rifle in his left hand. I stopped and Doak looked me over real careful before he waved for me to follow him.

Around the side of the shack he held a door open. Only a couple of wide planks nailed together and hung from a skinned pine log door jamb by two wide straps of leather, but the homespun build fit right in with the rest of the shanty. In the center of the one room stood a rough plank table surrounded by four three-legged stools. A stone fireplace on the north wall had a stick and mud chimney stained dark from smoke. Along the other three walls beds made from a log frame filled in with fresh pine needles covered by worn blankets sat on a bare dirt floor. Jeremiah lay in the bed at the rear of the room, and his right hand held a full-cocked pistol pointed straight at my chest. I stopped short, my hands wide.

"Put that gun down." Doak growled from a little behind my left shoulder.

But Jeremiah clung to the flintlock. "He's here to kill me Pa. He wants my girl."

"I told you to put the gun down." Doak thundered. "Ain't nobody getting shot in my house. I invited this boy in and he'll be treated like a guest should. You hear me, son?" Brawny and rough looking, in spite of the tunefulness of his low voice, Doak had the manner of a man you didn't want to rile.

Jeremiah's hand shook and I knew he must still be weak, yet he hung on to the pistol like a toddler does a rag doll. "I can't let him kill me, Pa. I can't."

"You put that gun down now, or whether the Good Lord will forgive me for it or not, I'll kill you myself." Doak bellowed at his son, his voice booming like a traveling preacher at a Sunday meeting, full of the fire and brimstone of the Lord.

"Damn, Pa—"

"Don't bring your words of Satan into my house, boy," Doak warned. "I'll throw you back into that gully and leave you for the buzzards. I won't have it I tell you. I won't have it. May the Good Lord strike me dead if I do."

Doak sure got out of sorts over a little bit of cussing, I thought. Eban said he walked the straight and narrow, but Doak's Sunday-go-to-meeting hollering worked on the gun-toting sinner, Jeremiah, and he let the hammer down real easy and pitched the pistol onto the dirt floor in front of his Pa. I wondered if the Wiggins' greeted all their guests with loaded firearms. Anyhow, I didn't feel too welcome right off.

Doak sat down on the fireplace side of the table and pointed at an empty stool across from him. "Sit boy. My son won't be shooting you today."

I took the offered stool, but looked around the room real careful to make sure there wasn't anybody else around pointing a gun at me. So far it's only a little after sun rise and I'd already had two guns aimed my way and still had to go to Coloma where more guys might take a notion to do the same. This chasing after Webster Lawson got awful exciting but it did have powerful drawbacks.

Jeremiah clutched a beat up brown blanket tight around his chest. Fear oozed from his eyes and washed across his tense, bruised face. It occurred to me that once K.O. Manuel realized Jeremiah was still alive he would likely be back to finish the job—and Jeremiah had to know that too.

"Tell him, Pa. Tell him what I told you." Jeremiah's voice held a tremble like Lacey's did before she burst out bawling, yet he still rang out with almost the same deep tone as Doak had, but with nowhere near the thunder of everlasting damnation.

"I told him," Doak answered. "He don't believe me and I don't blame him. You got to mend your own sins son. For once in your life tell the truth." Doak leaned out and scooped up the pistol Jeremiah had tossed over and stuck it in his waistband.

"He won't believe me either, Pa. You know that." Jeremiah pushed back closer to the wall and shivered like January.

I didn't have time for all this. I had to meet Eban. "Try me, Jeremiah," I said. "Your mind might boggle over what I'm willing to reckon on being the truth."

Jeremiah gulped, "It weren't me what shot you. Honest, it weren't me."

By now I already had a fair notion why Jeremiah cowered, but I wanted to hear it from his own lips. "All right, suppose you tell me what happened."

But instead of talking Jeremiah's gaze flitted around the room like he was watching a hummingbird dart from flower to flower. "Damn you boy!" Doak growled at him. "You got into this mess by your own doing. You didn't listen to your Pa or use the good sense I taught you. Now you only got one chance to save your black, rotten soul from the fires below. Tell this man the truth. That's what he come here for."

More hellfire and damnation, I thought, Doak was sure good at it.

"All right, Pa, all right," Jeremiah whined and looked down like he didn't want to see how I'd take to what he knew he had to say. "K.O. shot you," he admitted flat out. "He would have shot you earlier on the trail from Coloma but you must've changed your clothes and he wasn't sure it was you. So he drug me out of the Round Tent 'cause I knew you. Then he wanted me to shoot you, like a test, a loyalty test. He heard about our fight so he pushed me into it, threatened me, shamed me. I even had my rifle up, aimed right at you, but I couldn't pull the trigger. I just couldn't do it."

Jeremiah's eyes darted around the room again, but he pulled in a deep breath and kept talking. "K.O. slapped me around hard. He knocked me down then he shot you. You must've been awful lucky. K.O. don't miss much." Jeremiah shrank back even more, eyes wide, face pale and pulled at his blanket, clutching it even tighter to his chest.

"He didn't kill you," I noted.

Again Jeremiah's eyes danced around the room. "Yeah, reckon I'm lucky too," he said.

Somehow I took Jeremiah's words to heart. It made an odd kind of sense to me. "Why did you run then? I saw you heading down the road behind the wagon."

"K.O. ran up a dander something fierce that day." Jeremiah went on, his voice still trembling. "I never seen nobody get riled like he does. He killed a man in a bar fight once, just beat him to death after the poor man was already out cold. He's mean, I tell you, real mean. He started in on me again after he'd shot at you. I turned and ran like a rabbit the hounds jumped. After he saw you ride by the Round Tent he came after me again, and did this to my face."

And it came to me how the quiver in Lacey's voice couldn't hold a candle to Jeremiah's. The man in the red shirt had him totally spooked.

But I needed to get on with this. "Did K.O. kill those miners in Coloma?"

Jeremiah nodded then mumbled, "Yeah."

"Were you with him?"

"I held his horse. I didn't hurt nobody. I swear I didn't."

I thought now Jeremiah told me the gospel truth but one thing I still didn't understand at all. "Dang, Jeremiah, you knew this guy was a killer and you still partnered around with him. That don't make sense."

"I was scared, real scared, even before that, but he bought me these boots, then fed me brandy and gave me money, more than I'd ever seen. When they opened the office by the Round Tent all I had to do was tell him when somebody carped about getting cheated or when some Mexicans or Chinamen hit a big strike. I know I'm a fool. I know it."

That's something I could agree with. "Do you know Webster Lawson, the army fellow looking for your buddy K.O?" I asked, sure I'd hit the heart of things now.

"No, but K.O. knows him. They had a gunfight not long after K.O. killed one of the miners. K.O. thought he hit the army guy but got real mad when he got away. I told K.O. the guy would probably die soon, but I only did it to keep him from going over the edge like he does. I don't know what happened to him though, I swear I don't."

"Where was the gunfight?" Jeremiah was talking and I wanted to push him for anything that would help.

"We was past Coloma, near Weber Creek, maybe a mile south of the ford."

"Is that where K.O. camps?" I asked, knowing he had to hide out somewhere.

"No, he moved after that. He was north of the ford last time I was there. The water's too fast for mining and it's closer to the trail."

I stifled a snooty grin that itched to break across my face but might be misread by Jeremiah or his Pa. Now I knew exactly where K.O. camped. The time to go had come.

I got to my feet and turned to Doak. "Jeremiah's telling the truth, sir, but I'm right certain that when K.O. finds out he's alive he'll be back here. You'd best be ready for him, or maybe find a place to lay low a while. I got to ask you not to let on what you heard about these scalawags. Word could get back to them and they're liable to hightail it out of here and nobody will find them. Then Jeremiah ain't never going to be safe."

Doak stood. "We'll keep our mouths shut about your plans, my word on it. But I'll pray for that Godless spawn of Lucifer to show up here, 'cause I know the power of the Lord will smite him down like the black hearted rattlesnake he is. Praise the Lord."

Doak's right hand grabbed the handle of the flintlock pistol as he spoke and I wondered if that was the power of the Lord that Doak expected to smite K.O. Somehow I suspected it was. Still, I held out my hand. "Thank you, sir," I said.

Doak shook it. "Thank you, young man. I'll pray for you.

May the Good Lord guide and keep you on your dangerous task."

"Well, yes sir, I sure can use all the help I can get," I nodded towards Jeremiah and walked out the door and into the sunlight. This had gone way better than I'd hoped, better than I could have even dreamed.

I hopped on Rojo, splashed across the creek and dashed up the trail to the Coloma Road. Somewhere ahead of me Eban drove a freight wagon with the dun tied to the back. I should be able to catch him easy so I urged Rojo to run and the chestnut happily obliged. His hoof beats drummed in my ears, strong oaks swept past my eyes, a west wind whipped against my face, until, at the top of the hill half way to Coloma, I pulled up to give the horse a well-deserved breather.

After Rojo stopped I heard a rider coming fast from Coloma. The memory of K.O. passing me the last time I came by here flashed in my mind so I quickly slid into a patch of trees. When I got Rojo tucked behind some brush a man in a white straw hat wearing a red shirt and riding a pinto rose from the Coloma side of the hill. A shiver ran down my back. It was K.O. riding like the devil again. I hoped he wasn't heading to the Wiggins' place to finish what he started yesterday.

I stayed put long enough to let him get out of sight, then rode back onto the trail. Now I had a problem. Should I go after K.O. to help out Doak and Jeremiah or ride ahead to catch up with Eban? I knew Eban would be upset if I failed to show, but Doak Wiggins and his sons might be killed if K.O. showed up there. I didn't know what to do. But I wanted to go after K.O. It was the right thing to do. At least I thought so. Still, I'd made a promise to Eban and a man's word was his bond, that's what Pa taught me. I pranced Rojo first north then south, my mind a jumble of uncertainty.

A shout came from the north, faint and muffled by the hill, but clearly a man and somehow familiar. It came again, louder. I nudged Rojo toward Coloma. At the edge of the clearing the cry came once more. "Hiyah! Get on mules. Get on now." It was Eban coming this way. I tore down the trail to meet him.

Around the first turn the freight wagon, with the dun tied to the rear, raced uphill as fast as Eban could drive the team. I pulled back on Rojo's reins so hard the chestnut reared up on his hind legs. I yanked off the sombrero and waved. Eban waved back and I edged to the side of the trail so the wagon wouldn't have to stop. After it passed I turned Rojo to catch up.

When I came alongside Eban looked over. "That was the man we're looking for, wasn't it?" he asked in strained voice.

"Yeah, that's him," I said. "I'm betting he's heading back to finish the job on Jeremiah. Somebody must've told K.O. that he wasn't dead. We need to help."

"Who would've told a miscreant like him something like that?" Eban asked as he struggled to turn the mules a bit so the wagon wouldn't ride over a deep rut.

"I don't know, Reid Harrison, I guess."

"Okay, reckon you might be right." Eban yanked the reins in the other direction.

I stood up tall in the stirrups. "I know where K.O.'s camp is." I crowed, pleased that I'd pulled this information out of Jeremiah and wanting Eban to know about it.

"That's good, but right now he ain't heading to his camp," Eban pointed out.

"Yeah, you're right. Shouldn't we hurry up and catch up to him, otherwise Jeremiah and Doak are liable to get killed," I pled.

Eban pondered a bit. "Son, we ain't going to do any good chasing this feller. What we need to do is find Webster Lawson like we started out doing," he finally said.

"But Eban—"

"No buts. Now listen to me. First we ain't lawmen, and second, if I know Doak Wiggins, he don't need much help. I'd bet he's got a plan and he's ready. Am I right?"

"Yeah, Eban, you're right." I had to admit it. "He even said he wanted K.O. to show up at his shack."

"Yeah, well, while the cat's away the mice can play. How about you and me see what kind of goodies we can dig up in Coloma while old K.O. Manuel is busy somewhere else?" Eban grinned big and pulled the rig off the trail to turn it around in the clearing.

"Are you sure about this, Eban?" I asked, not sure of anything myself.

"Well, to tell the truth I ain't sure, but a man's got to take some chances in life. It don't look like we can do Doak Wiggins much good, and that sidewinder on the pinto might not be heading to Doak's place anyhow. I mean, we don't know he's after Jeremiah right now do we?" Eban said and I knew he had a point.

"I'll sure feel bad if we're wrong about it." I said and my

head drooped some. I'd taken a shine to Doak Wiggins and didn't want him hurt.

"I'll be as sorry as you are. Doak's a fine man. Can't say the same for Jeremiah, but Doak's upstanding and honest. Ain't enough men like him anymore." Suddenly Eban took on a puzzled look. "How come that K.O. scalawag didn't see you on the trail?" he asked. "You was here weren't you?"

I gave a small groan. "I heard him coming and slipped off into the trees." I nodded toward the clump of oaks where I'd hid, but it came to me how lucky I'd been, again. If K.O. had come over the hill just a little sooner I wouldn't have heard him over the pounding of Rojo's hooves. If he'd seen me first I might be dead now. I looked up and gave a silent thank you. Like I'd told Doak, I could use all the help I could get.

Meantime Eban stopped the wagon and peered back in the direction K.O. had ridden. He scratched his chin whiskers like he did when he mulled things over. Soon he turned to me. "Was that scoundrel riding fast when he passed here?" he asked.

"Yeah, he rode by like a whole tribe of Comanche was after him."

"He passed me near that curve where you found me. Then he rode slow, like he didn't have a care in the world, and eyeballed me hard like he was looking for somebody. I heard him rouse the pinto when he got out of my sight so I turned around as soon as I could, worried about you." Eban said. He whipped the reins and the mules slowly lumbered off toward Coloma.

But I sat stock still on Rojo and stared down the trail toward Hangtown Creek. Another steaming June day heated up but I wrapped my arms around my chest and shivered with a chill that shook my whole body. "Eban!" I yelled, "You're right! K.O. ain't after Jeremiah—he's after me."

"Whoa." The wagon stopped and Eban looked back, eyebrows raised. "What else did you find out from Jeremiah Wiggins, son?" he asked.

"Jeremiah didn't shoot at me. K.O. Manuel did."

Eban didn't take long to ponder what I'd said. He cracked the reins hard. "Let's go," he hollered. "We got no time to waste." He cracked the reins again. "Get up mules! Hiyah, get on now." The rig sped up quick as it headed downhill.

##

The wagon rolled down Coloma's main street. I trailed behind. When I passed the Golden Nugget Saloon, with the California Mining Cooperative office of Frank Barney next door, I ducked down to hide my face behind the broad brim of the sombrero. Even though K.O. Manuel had left town I didn't want anyone to see me. If Frank Barney, or someone else who knew me from the time I spent here last summer, told K.O. that I was in town I might be shot, maybe killed, a thought that churned my gut raw.

Still, I stayed mindful that Jeremiah said he got his fancy boots for hanging around the Round Tent Saloon and telling on anybody who carped about the mining cooperative. It stood to reason there might be another fellow here in Coloma who wore a fancy pair of Mexican boots that didn't match his homemade hand-me-down pants. I resolved to keep a heedful eye out for that somebody, but only when I felt safe from the prying eyes of those who might want to do me harm.

When I turned into the saw mill lot someone raced by me on foot, chasing the freight wagon. "Load your wagon for you, mister? Only a dollar," he yelled. Boyd Riddle loped along in the head bobbing, arm waving way he had, set on getting to Eban before anyone else did. I pushed Rojo to a trot and followed.

Eban stopped in front of a pile of lumber. He climbed to the ground and looked straight at Boyd. "How are you, son," he said when Boyd got within easy earshot.

"I'm right fine, sir. Nice to see you again," Boyd gasped. He put his left hand on his waist and caught his breath, but his head still wobbled back and forth.

Eban moved to the back of the wagon and untied the dun. "It's Boyd, ain't it?"

"Yes, sir."

"Well, Boyd, can you handle the whole load yourself? I got some things to do." Eban sounded like a man in a hurry.

"Oh, I can handle it real easy," Boyd agreed.

I pulled Rojo to a stop a few paces behind Boyd. "I give him two dollars for the whole load, Eban." I wanted to help my friend.

Boyd spun around and grinned. "Tom! Howdy. Sakes alive, you look different every time I see you. I thought you was a Mexican feller and ran right by you. Are you two together?"

"Yeah, we are." I said. "Say Boyd, could you answer a question for me?"

"Sure, be happy to."

"It came to me watching you run over here and just might be real important to us."

Behind Boyd Eban scratched his whiskers, uncertainty whittled deep into his face.

But I kept talking to Boyd, "Last time I saw you, you mentioned a fellow near your camp who talked about the miners' cooperative running folks off claims. Was that guy a gold panner?"

Boyd looked down and pulled on his earlobe. "As I recall he dressed real nice, like you, all in store bought clothes and such. He didn't look like no miner to me."

My mind raced. "Do you recall what he did look like?" I asked.

Boyd rolled his eyes up some before he went on. "I recollect him right good. He was a tall, lanky feller, with a skinny moustache and one of them scrawny chin beards. He had some awful thick eyebrows too. Seems like he was losing his hair, but I could be wrong about that. He dressed a lot like one of them fresh-off-the-boat fellers too."

I hardly believed my ears. "Do you know where he camped? Eban and me sure would like to talk to him." The man Boyd saw sounded exactly like Lacey's pa.

Boyd pulled on his earlobe one more time, looked upriver and wagged a finger. "It was right after sunup when he stopped by heading west, down this way. He must've camped somewhere close to Pa and me. Don't know if he's still there or not. That was soon after them three guys got killed. Ain't seen him but that one time."

I needed a little more. "Where's your camp?"

Again Boyd pointed upstream. "You know the ford that leads to the dry diggings on the other side of the river?" he asked.

"Yeah, I know it." I frowned. I knew the ford well.

"We're across the river at the top of the first ravine to the east. Pa ought to be there. He might even be doing a little mining, if he's feeling up to it."

"I'm glad he's doing better, Boyd," I said with all honesty.

Eban stepped up from the back of the wagon, leading the dun. "Boyd, what would you say to three dollars for helping the two of us load the wagon then, when we're done, you take us over to where you think this guy camped?"

Boyd's mouth opened wide before breaking into a broad grin. "Yes sir," he agreed right quick. "I'd say that's powerful generous of you, downright kindly."

"Good, let's get to it. We got no time to dilly-dally," Eban said and looked over to me. "Is this alright with you, son?"

"You bet it is." I rippled with excitement. If I came home and told Lacey that I'd found her Pa she'd be flat out tickled pink.

Eban led the dun to the millrace and left him to drink his fill and graze in the tall grass there. I followed with Rojo. Then we all pitched in to make short work loading the pile of lumber onto the wagon.

We left the rig in the saw mill lot, picked up Boyd's old mare from the hitching post in front of the blacksmith shop and headed east past the road to Hangtown Creek. At the ford across the American River I got another cold chill up my backbone. It was a good bet that somewhere close to here Scarface and his partner killed my two brothers to steal the supplies on their mule. As far as I knew nobody had ever seen a trace of Hank, but the body of poor Jess washed up by the millrace dam the next morning and my life changed forever.

When we reached the north bank we turned right and headed upstream. A lot of men worked here. Some stood in the river and panned ore while others dug in one of the gulches that carried the rainwater to the river in the wet winter months. At the bottom of these ravines, in a layer of clay just above the bedrock, men often found nuggets as big as a robin's egg. A man who mined in the right spot could become rich in weeks.

Before the first ravine Boyd stopped the mare at a rocky pathway that led up the side of the river valley. "That feller you're looking for, if he's the same one I talked to, must've camped somewhere up on the ridgeline. All the good mining spots near the water have men working claims. But further up, away from the river, a man's got to carry the ore to the water to pan. It's a lot of work and I don't know what anybody's found much color near the top anyhow."

He pointed to the path, nothing more than hoof prints in the dirt. "This leads up to a game trail along the ridge. From there we can look down into the ravines. Maybe we can spot this feller's campsite, if he's still around."

Eban nodded. "It's worth a try," he said and started up the hill.

We took the path single file. I brought up the rear. Rojo easily picked his way through the brush, scrub oak, stones and rocks that littered the way. He'd spent his early days as a cow horse. Trained by Mexican vaqueros, he acted right at home in the rugged gold country.

Near the top of the slope, I looked down to the American River. From here it seemed a calm, gentle stream and not the roaring torrent that it did below. The ripples and eddies, caused when the powerful current broke over rocks or washed past snags as the river swept onward to Sacramento City, weren't so clear anymore. But all along the stream men still stood in the water panning for color, and shacks and shanties like the one Doak Wiggins lived in were scattered across the shore. The river here was a busy place.

Boyd pointed to a man sitting on the hillside off to our right, wooden splints lashed to his left leg, who chopped the soil near the top of the ravine with a small ax, pulled the dirt out with his hands and pawed through it looking for nuggets. "That's my Pa," he said, shaking his head. "There ain't no gold up this high on the hill, leastwise nobody's found none yet, but he digs anyway. He can't hardly walk, but every day he works at his digging, bound and determined, and never finds a single nugget."

The sadness in Boyd's voice came across clear, but something about his Pa didn't make much sense. "Why don't you move to a place where you'd be more apt to find gold?" I asked.

"I talked to him till I was blue in the face, but he don't listen," Boyd said. "He's dead set on the idea that all the gold they find down near the river comes from up here. Says it all must wash downhill and swears he'll find a big pocket soon. Been saying that since we moved here, right after his leg broke. I don't know, maybe he's right." Boyd looked down, clucked at the mare and rode off across the ridge.

I watched the tall, gangly farm boy riding ahead of me. Boyd loaded wagons, worked hard at whatever job he could find, all so his Pa could search for gold, even in a place where there wasn't any to be found. That took a special sort of man, somebody with a big heart packed with love. I'd always felt pretty dang good about giving Boyd money for loading the wagon. Now I knew why.

We rode on past the start of several other ravines that grew wider as they went downhill, but no one else camped along any of them. All around only dry grass and scrub brush grew in the bare, hard ground. We saw no water, no shade and no good place for a man to camp. If Webster Lawson was still here I sure couldn't figure out why, but Boyd kept going, like he knew where he headed and so we trailed along behind.

Finally the country changed. Pine trees grew along the ridge again, lone oaks on the slope. Boyd stopped and nodded to a small clump of bay trees surrounded by brush at the top of a ravine that zigzagged back and forth as it grew wider on the way to the river. "If the feller you're looking for is around. That's the likely spot."

Eban grinned a bit and scratched his chin. "Any water there?"

Boyd shrugged. "Don't know. Bay trees like water but there ain't none running down the gully right now."

I nudged Rojo. "There's only one way to find out if Lacey's pa is there," I called back and hustled down the hill.

"Hold on, Tom." Eban yelled. "We don't know who might be in there."

"We know K.O. ain't there. Come on." Webster Lawson could easily be in those trees. I had set my mind to find him like Boyd's pa had set his to find gold. I wasn't about to wait for anybody or anything. The clatter of horses came from behind me. Eban and Boyd followed.

A sickening stink twitched my nose. It got stronger closer to the trees. Something foul sat somewhere in that grove. I gulped. Anything could be behind those bushes in a spot this out of the way, but I sure didn't want to have to tell Lacey I'd found her pa dead and rotting. I pulled up my bandana and wrapped it tight around my mouth and nose hoping to block the stench. It didn't help much. At the edge of the brush I stopped Rojo and climbed to the ground.

"Take that scattergun with you," Eban yelled from behind me.

I glanced back at him. He wore a no-nonsense, worried look, and I quickly pulled the shotgun from the scabbard. With it in my hand I felt better right off. After all, I still didn't know what was under the trees. A huge grizzly bear or a fierce mountain lion might lurk there, ready to protect its supper of a deer. Or it could be the body of Webster Lawson, dead from the gunfight with K.O. Manuel. I found a likely place to push through the bushes and paused.

"Be careful Tom," Eban hollered after me, then in a softer voice I heard him add, "You wait here, Boyd. No use you putting up with this stink."

A fierce quiver shook me all over. My heart thumped fast inside like it had after K.O. shot Jeremiah yesterday. I tried to take a deep breath but gagged from the smell, so I put my free hand on the bandana and sucked in some air through my mouth. It was still pretty foul. I cocked one barrel of the shotgun, put my shoulder down and charged into the brush.

A horrible squawking broke out. I grabbed the scattergun in both hands, finger on the trigger, and burst into the clearing. Shrieks and a loud whooping sound rose up. An ugly, shriveled red head with bulging, beady eyes loomed in front of me. Toppling backwards I yelled and jerked the trigger. The shotgun went off with a boom that would wake the dead and a kick that knocked me flat on my rump. More squawks, more whooping and another monster came right at me, talons bloody, raw meat hanging from its beak. I screamed again, rolled over on my belly and covered my head with my hands, knocking the sombrero off as I did. Whatever bird just attacked me had to be the most hideous, fearsome critter I'd ever laid eyes on.

"Tom, you all right?" Eban called. He sounded as scared as I felt.

"I'm okay, I think," I yelled back, and realized that the squawking had stopped. I pulled my hands down and peeked back where the last ugly, redheaded monster jumped me. Everything seemed calm, quiet even, with no sign of any monster all. I grabbed my sombrero and the shotgun, stood up and walked carefully back into the clearing. At once I saw the source of the smell. It looked like a horse, or what had once been a horse. It wasn't a pretty sight. The bile in my gut rose, but I swallowed hard and managed to keep it down.

A man lay on a bedroll to my left and pointed a pistol right at me. That made three today, I thought. The man's hand shook worse than Jeremiah's had earlier, and he was as pale as anybody I'd ever seen. Plus he had a bloody, yellow bandana tied around his left thigh. It didn't take a lot of deducting to know who he was. "You're Webster Lawson, ain't you," I said.

"Who're you?" he said in a weak, squeaky voice.

"Name's Tom Marsh. I'm here to help you if I can. Lacey's

awful worried over you, sir, but I'd worry a lot less if you'd put that pistol down." I yanked the bandana off my face and wrinkled up the brightest smile I could muster at the moment, but I was getting awful tired of people pointing guns in my direction.

"Lacey? You know Lacey?" The gun sagged to the ground.

"Yes, sir. I know her right good."

Lawson's eyes flicked toward the brush behind me. "Who's with you?"

Eban stepped into the clearing, a rifle cradled in one arm. "Name's Snyder, Major Lawson, Eban Snyder," he said and touched the brim of his straw hat.

"How do you know me, Snyder?" Lawson sounded so hoarse he crackled.

"The war, sir. Hauled a lot of supplies for Fremont under your orders."

"Yeah, I guess you would've." He wheezed and laid his head back against the saddle he used as a pillow. "Do you have water?"

Eban nodded. "I'll get my canteen," he said and ducked back through the brush.

I had to ask, "Are you alright, sir? I mean why are you here like this?"

"It's a long story. Will you help me sit up, son?"

"Sure," I answered and walked over, took the Major's hand and pulled him up. Off to my left a rocky hole, still wet along the bottom, must have held water recently. A tin cup jammed against the high side caught a slow drip that had probably been Webster Lawson's only supply of fresh water for a while.

"Thanks," the Major whispered. He braced himself with one hand, hung his head and sighed. "If you hadn't shown up they would've started in on me as soon as they finished with my horse." He gave a weak wave around the clearing with the other hand.

"They, sir?" I thought he had to be talking about the monsters that attacked me. After all, he must've seen them.

"Vultures, the vilest creature God ever made. They've been here since yesterday and I've already made my peace with the Good Lord." He managed a weak smile. "You hit the one you shot at. Blew him way over there. Good riddance." Lacey's Pa nodded toward the brush across from where I'd come into the clearing.

Vultures! I could slap myself. I should've known, but I'd never seen one so close before, never had the slightest notion that any of God's creations could look so down right wicked. The thought of being so near to something that would eat the dead, stinking flesh of the horse turned my stomach again. This time I couldn't hold it down. I ran to the bushes and heaved.

When I finished I wiped my mouth and turned around. Eban had made it back and now he stared at me with a smug grin across his face. I hung my head, red faced that I'd lost my breakfast like I'd done and that Eban had seen it. I needed to be tougher. I knew it. He was bound to take me to task about it now.

But he turned instead to Lacey's pa who still sucked on the canteen Eban had gotten for him. "We need to get out of here, Major. I got a crawling in my gut too. Can you ride?"

Lawson wiped his mouth with his sleeve and handed the canteen back. "Thanks," he said. "I can probably ride, but I can't walk. I took a ball in the leg."

"I'll look at it, but right now I'd feel better if we got away from this stench." Eban helped Lacey's pa to his feet and wrapped the Major's left arm over his shoulder. Together they hobbled through the brush to the horses.

While I waited for them I rolled up Webster Lawson's bedroll and slung it across my back, picked up his saddle and saddlebags and followed them. I caught up outside the clearing. Rojo stood a lot closer than the dun and I untied the reins. "You can ride my horse, Major. I'll walk alongside. We can go to Boyd's camp and figure out what to do next."

Both men looked at me with raised eyebrows, but Eban grinned. "So you're in charge of this operation now, are you, Tom?" he asked.

I dropped the saddle and flopped the bedroll and saddlebags onto Rojo. "I'm only trying to help, Eban," I mumbled like any kid would who'd just been chided for acting uppity to his elders.

Lacey's pa put a hand on my shoulder. "And you're doing a fine job, Tom. I owe you my life, young man, and I humbly accept your generous offer to let me ride your horse." His voice still crackled a little but he sounded a lot smoother now that he'd had some water. I looked up, surprised to see a smile on his face. I grinned back, feeling better, and together Eban and I had Web Lawson mounted on the chestnut in no time.

Eban picked up the Major's saddle. "We'd best get on with this. Them vultures circling over our heads look real ornery," he declared to no one's surprise.

While Eban climbed on the dun, I took Rojo's reins and walked off toward Boyd who waited up at the ridgeline. Lacey's pa sat quiet in the saddle, slumped down low, eyes sunken and closed, beard growing wild over gray, ghostly skin. In the sunlight I could see how thin he looked. His clothes hung loose like they belonged to somebody a lot bigger.

When we got near Boyd's camp, I looked back again to check on the Major. His eyes were open now. "Are you okay, sir?" I asked.

Webster Lawson nodded. "I'm awful hungry, son," he moaned.

I grinned. "You're in luck, sir. I packed enough food to last all of us a couple of days. When we get to camp I'll whip you up some pan bread for starters, then I'll see what else I can put together for you."

A sparkle flashed in Major Lawson's eyes, though he still looked weak and pale. "That's fine, Tom. Thank you." He took a deep breath and coughed. "You mentioned Lacey, how do you know my little girl? Are you from San Francisco?"

"Oh, no sir. Eban and me live over the hill along Hangtown Creek." I pointed off to the south. "Lacey came up to Coloma a few days ago. Mrs. Wimmer rounded her up about the time Eban stopped by to get Mrs. Wimmer to help Maggie with her new baby, so Lacey came along. She's a big help with baby Josie and down at the cafe. She stays up at the cabin with Maggie." I looked square into the Major's face and continued. "Lacey's awful worried about you, sir."

Major Lawson's gray face darkened. "I told her to stay put," he groused. "Why did she leave home?"

I felt my eyebrows knot together as my mouth twisted up some. The Major sounded mad now and he'd asked a tough question that I didn't know how to answer. Still, I had to try. "She said some fellow there scared her real bad, sir. But when it comes right down to it, I'd say she missed you a whole bunch."

Lacey's pa shook his head softly. "She's always been too headstrong for her own good. I guess I should thank God she found people like you and Eban to take care of her."

"Oh, no sir, nobody's taking care of her, she holds her own pretty darn good. Yesterday she cooked lunch and dinner at the cafe and the miners loved it."

"Yeah, she can cook, that's a fact. And right now I'd give a month's pay for some of her roast chicken and giblet gravy."

My grin came back. I'd loved the chicken and gravy too.

"Later you'll have to tell me more about this cafe you're so fond of," he added.

Then I heard Boyd Riddle cry out, "Pa, we're going to have company tonight."

Boyd's pa turned from where he sat at the top of the ravine. Instead of looking at his son he stared straight at Webster Lawson and nodded, like they knew each other. "That's just fine," he said in a flat, dry tone that didn't have a thimbleful of feeling to it. He turned back to the river and swung the hatchet into the hard packed earth again and again, bent only on the gold he sought.

I led Rojo toward where Eban waited, sitting on the dun ahead of me near a small stand of pines that crept across the ridge. "I've got to get that load of lumber delivered,' he said. "I'll give you a hand getting the Major settled and we've got to go."

The idea of going to Hangtown rattled my mind almost like the vultures had. K.O. Manuel might be out there somewhere waiting to shoot me as I rode back with Eban and the wagon. In the stir around finding Lacey's pa I'd forgotten all about the man in the red shirt, but now I recalled how lucky I'd been so far and knew that luck wouldn't hold up forever. "I'm going to stay here, Eban, if it's all right with Boyd." I muttered. "I promised to cook some pan bread for Major Lawson anyway. He's real hungry."

With a pained look across his face, Eban shook his head hard from side to side. "No, Tom!" he snapped. "If something happened to you while I wasn't here, so many folks would be after me I'd have more holes in my carcass than one of Maggie's pincushions."

"But Eban, K.O. might be waiting—"

"K.O. Manuel?" It was Lacey's pa, interrupting in a voice stronger than he'd shown before. "How do you know him?"

I shrugged. "Well sir, he wants to kill me. He shot at me day before yesterday," I yanked off the sombrero, "See," and pointed to the scab on my head. "But he missed. This morning a fellow who was there told me it was him. Then later today, on the trail here, I heard K.O. riding like the devil, heading towards Hangtown, so I hid in the brush. I think he was looking for me."

The Major shook his head and turned to Eban. "If K.O. Manuel wants someone dead, he usually gets what he wants. He could easily be waiting on that trail for Tom to ride back. No one knows Tom is here. He'd be better off to stay."

I gulped. Hearing the Major say what he did caused a chill to run right through me.

It must have scared Eban too. He gave a little jump in the saddle that made the dun take two quick sideways steps to the left. "Whoa, boy, whoa," he yelled. The horse stopped and Eban looked at the Major. "So you know this Manuel feller?" he asked.

"Only by reputation, but he's a bad character, real bad." Major Lawson turned back to me. "He's the one that put this hole in my leg. Did he snipe at you from the trailside, son?"

"Yes sir. He would've killed me if I hadn't been lucky." My eyes stared down at the top of my beat up boots while my feet shuffled nervously in the dust.

The Major inhaled with a wheeze, "Well there you have it," he said to Eban. "Tom has already been ambushed along that trail. It would be stupid for him to go there again. In my opinion he'd be safer here."

"You bet he'd be safer here." The yell came from my left. I turned to see Boyd's pa leaning on a homemade crutch at the top of the ravine, waving a large bore Hawken rifle in his other hand. "I'll blow that lowdown rattlesnake straight to hell if he comes across the river. You bring me a Bible and I'll swear in front of God that there won't be no harm come to the boy or the Major as long as I'm here. You can count on the word of Bug Riddle. I ain't never gone back on a sworn oath and I ain't going to now." Boyd's pa held up the heavy rifle and pumped it into the air, wobbling back and forth on the crutch as he did. "Bring me a Bible so I can swear. Bring it you hear," he yelled to Boyd.

"Pa, take it easy now," Boyd cried. "Ain't no use for you to get so riled, we all believe you." He jumped down from the mare and rushed to his pa. "Why don't you sit back down? All this hopping around ain't good for your leg." He took the rifle and crutch and helped his pa sit where he could keep on with his digging.

Eban scratched his chin and looked back to me. "Sounds like the Major's on your side, son, and so is Mr. Riddle." He sighed real loud then went on, "I'll figure out something to tell the women. Meanwhile you keep out of sight. I'll be back tomorrow."

Boyd walked up to us after he'd had gotten his pa settled. "I reckon I ought to apologize for Pa. He ain't been right since he busted that leg. That's when he wanted to camp here. Now he sits there every day digging in the dirt, and always with that bear gun beside him. I do what I can." Boyd shook his head.

I had to ask, "Is his name really Bug?"

Boyd nodded, "Yeah, leastwise that's what folks call him. They say he's like one of them pesky little gnats back east. Once they latch on to you, you can't get shed of them. That's how he is. Gets a notion in his head and just keeps at it."

Eban gave the dun a nudge. "Well, I got to get back over the hill before sundown. What say we get you settled, Major, and I'll take a look at that leg before I go."

I handed Rojo's reins up to the Major. "Will you be okay, sir?" I asked.

"I can make it, son," Web Lawson took the leather straps in his left hand and followed Eban to the pines that nosed over the ridge.

At the top of the ravine Bug Riddle chopped at the dirt again with the small hand ax, his eyes still honed in on the ford where we had crossed the river and looking for all the world like he was waiting for somebody special. I wondered who that somebody could be as I walked over to him.

"Hi, Mr. Riddle. My name's Tom Marsh. I want to thank you for letting us stay at your camp," I said and squatted down on my haunches beside him.

Bug looked over at me through bitter, sad eyes. "You're right welcome," he mumbled and took another random hack at the bare earth with the ax before he looked back to the river like he didn't want to talk. He had on a battered brown hat with a hole worn through the crown and a brim that had long ago lost any hint of its original shape, going up in some places and down in others for no reason. Frayed green suspenders strapped over a faded blue shirt held up ragged homemade pants so caked with the dirt he dug day after day that they seemed to be a part of the hillside.

But I wasn't about to let things go so easy. There was something about Bug Riddle, something I couldn't wrap my mind around, something important. "I don't know how much you know about our, ah, well, our problem, sir, but it could be dangerous for you to have us here. You need to know that," I explained, figuring he had a right to the truth about why we were here.

Bug hacked at the earth again, eyes still trained off in the distance. "You're the one my boy loads wagons for," he said kind of quiet and unexpected like. "He likes you. Say's you're good folk. That's all that matters. Good people got to band together against that black-hearted son of Satan. He ruins all he touches, brings suffering and death to everybody he meets." The ax slammed into hard clay again and again and again.

I wasn't quite sure who the black-hearted son of Satan that Bug Riddle talked about was exactly, but I understood the difference between good people and bad people real clear now. K.O. Manuel and his cronies were definitely bad ones and guys like Boyd were as good as a man could find, and even if Bug sounded a little off his feed right now, I was dang sure he must be good too.

I got to my feet. "I'm planning on fixing something to eat, sir. Are you hungry?" I asked.

Bug Riddle didn't look up. He kept his hard gaze on the river and continued to chop at the earth. "Don't you worry, son," he assured me. "I'll put a ball through that red shirted spawn of Lucifer as soon as he rides into the river. I'll blow him back to Hades where he belongs and good riddance to him." And then he spat off toward the water.

My eyes were wide now. Even though Bug Riddle sounded like the apples fell off his tree way too early he'd used almost the exact same words that Doak Wiggins had used to describe K.O. Manuel. Still, I was a guest here and didn't want to wear out my welcome right off by asking all the questions that he'd just provoked in me. "I'll come back when the food is done, sir." I offered instead and didn't wait for him to answer but hurried up to the ridge where smoke already rose from a small campfire.

My mind churned, chock-full of thoughts from my short talk with Bug Riddle. One thing stood out clear. Bug was powerful mad at somebody he called a red shirted spawn of Lucifer—the devil's child in a red shirt. I'd bet Maggie's chestnut horse against a horny toad that Bug Riddle was talking about K.O. Manuel, and doing it just like Doak Wiggins had.

Eban walked up to me, leading the dun. "The Major's leg is healing up fine but the ball's still inside. Mostly he's suffering from too little food and water. If you feed him good he'll be okay. He asked me not to tell Lacey that we found him. He's afraid she'll hightail it over here and get herself in trouble. But I'm more worried about you. Are you sure you'll be alright here?"

"Yeah, Eban. K.O. doesn't know where I am. Major Lawson's right. I'd be in a lot more danger on the trail," I said, knowing Eban had good reason to be fretful.

He swung into the saddle. "I'll be back tomorrow, as early as I can get here. Meantime you stay close to camp and take care of yourself."

"I will, Eban." I promised, then stood and watched as he rode down the hill, crossed the river and swung west toward the Hangtown Road.

When I turned back to the ridge I saw Boyd bracing pine branches against a log and snapping them in half with his boot so he could burn them in the campfire he was building. "I know my Pa sounds loco," he said without looking up. "He's been like that since he broke his leg. Just sits and watches the river. Says he's looking for gold, but he ain't, not really. Something happened to him, something bad, but he won't talk about it."

What Boyd said boiled together in my mind with what Bug told me earlier like meat and potatoes in Maggie's stews. Somewhere a bell rang as clear as the one on the cafe door. "Were you camped on Weber Creek, maybe a mile south of the ford, when your Pa broke his leg?"

Boyd's jaw dropped. "Did Pa tell you that?"

"No, it's a guess. What happened? Did you see him break it?"

Boyd stomped on another piece of pine. It snapped in half with a pop. "No, I was panning ore downstream when Pa's hat come floating by me. The creek runs pretty fast and deep there, but I sloshed out and grabbed it. I knew I'd never hear the end of things if Pa lost that hat. Then here he comes washing down after it, arms flailing, gasping for air, face beat to a pulp. He was half drowned by the time I got him out of the river. I had to pump on his chest to get all the water out of him. Then, after I lugged him back to camp, I found out that the horses ran off and I had to chase one down before I could get Pa to town. He said he slipped and the leg broke. But that ain't what it looked like to me." Boyd looked down, a frown across his face.

But my ears had perked up. "How long after the three miners got killed?"

Boyd scratched his cheek. "Oh, a day or so after the last guy, not long."

"And they got killed real near where you and your Pa were camped when his leg broke, didn't they?"

"Yeah, the two Mexicans was shot just downstream. The old fellow got beat to death a day or two before that. He weren't too far upstream. How do you know all this? You wasn't there?" Boyd shot back, his eyes wide with wonderment.

"No, but I think the man that shot the Major and took a pot shot at me Monday is the same fellow who broke your Pa's leg then likely tossed him into the creek to drown. I can see why your Pa's mad. I fell off my horse at the Weber Creek ford a year ago, got washed downstream and near died from it. It's something that sticks with me, and nobody broke my leg and threw me in."

"Sounds like something I been thinking on for a while, but when I ask Pa about it he tells me to mind my own business," Boyd admitted, sadness in his voice.

"Yeah, I suppose he would." I looked back toward Bug Riddle. "How did he get that fancy rifle," A Hawken cost a lot of money and Boyd and Bug didn't seem like they'd ever had much.

"He won it in a shooting match back in Tennessee when I was a boy. It's his pride and joy. There ain't many who could outshoot him then and that rifle's the proof." Boyd said it real plain and I knew he wasn't just putting a good face on his pa. He really meant it. Then he stood. "Speaking of shooting," he went on. "How about I slip over the hill and see if I can bag a rabbit or two? I'm a pretty fair shot myself."

"You bet!" I exclaimed. "That sounds great." Jess shot a lot of wild critters back on the farm but since I'd been in the gold country I'd mostly been eating beef, pork, a little deer and a lot of chicken. Fresh rabbit would be a treat.

Boyd picked up a small-bore rifle and headed over the ridge. I walked to Rojo for my saddlebags. The horse grazed close to where Lacey's Pa rested on his bedroll.

He watched me as I neared. "I heard your talk with Bug Riddle and the questions you asked Boyd. You put things together real good, son, and fast too," he said in a low, quiet way like he didn't want anybody else to hear him.

I even glanced back to the ravine to see if Bug listened, but Boyd's pa sat in the same spot, still hacking at the ground with his hatchet. "One thing seemed to follow another, sir," I said. "I mean how many bad men can there be around here anyhow?"

"More than you might think, I'm afraid, but none as bad as K.O. Manuel. You and I need to have a serious talk, Tom, maybe after that pan bread you promised." The Major gave a little smile then coughed.

"I'll get you some food, sir, as soon as I can," I said with a grin and hurried back to the campfire with the saddlebags.

I knelt by the fire pit, well made with flat stones on three sides to hold in the heat. It would be easy to whip up pan bread here. Soon salt pork sizzled in the pan and I had four balls of dough ready to flatten down and fry up. I tossed the first one into to the grease. When it browned on the bottom I flipped it into the air and caught it raw side down in the pan, a perfect flapjack. After it was done I took it over to the Major, along with some of the bacon and a cup of coffee.

"Thank you, son." he said as he took the tin plate from me. "This smells absolutely fantastic." He broke off a chunk and popped it into his mouth.

"I'm sorry we got no butter or molasses, sir. It helps."

A shot rang out from the backside of the ridge. Almost like magic Major Lawson's hand flew up holding his Colt. I quickly spun toward where the sound came from but didn't see anything odd so I turned back to the river. Bug Riddle sat at the top of the ravine, chopping the earth with his ax like nothing had happened.

"That shot must have come from Boyd," I said. "I hope he bagged a rabbit."

The Major gasped and his hand dropped to the ground, but he kept a grip on the pistol. It was a Paterson Colt, a revolver like a whole bunch of those fresh-off-the-boat miners carried. The Major was well armed.

His head rested back onto his saddle and his eyes closed. He still held the bread in his other hand, but he wasn't even trying to eat now. Maybe somebody shot the Major, I worried. But as soon as the thought formed his eyes fluttered open and he gave a weak smile.

"I guess today has been a little more than I've been used to," he said softly. "I'll eat your bread, son, with or without butter and I'll enjoy every bite."

I grinned. "I know you're real hungry, sir, but I've heard that you need to eat slow when you haven't had any food in a while. You might get sick or something."

"I'll eat slow," he said, then his gaze strayed to the top of the ravine. "Maybe you should offer our host some."

"Oh, yes sir. I'll make enough for all of us, and I can always make more."

"That's good," he whispered and his eyes closed again.

I thought it best to leave him alone for a while, so I went back to the fire and cooked up more pan bread and headed to the ravine with it. When I got close Bug threw down his ax and grabbed the Hawken, ready to pull it to his shoulder. I looked to the ford and saw what sparked the old man's interest. Someone in a dark blue shirt, a black hat and riding a pinto splashed into the stream.

From this far above the river the rider looked a lot like K.O. Manuel, yet something didn't seem right. It wasn't the shirt or the hat. K.O. could have more than one of those. I reflected back on the man I'd seen only a few times and only at a quick glance. But Bug raised the Hawken, cocked the hammer and sniffed up a deep breath. He was going to shoot.

"No," I yelled. "Don't fire. That ain't him."

"That's his pinto," Bug snarled.

"I don't think so. His pinto had a brown left foreleg. That one's white. Besides K.O. Manuel has his hair cut short, this guy's got long hair. Look at him close."

Bug stared hard then eased the hammer down. "You know him?" he asked, not saying who he thought the guy was but I knew now he waited here for K.O.

"No, but I've seen him a couple of times," I said. "He tried to kill me."

The man on the pinto rode out of the stream, turned east and continued along the riverbank, his long black locks flowed out from under his hat and a guitar hung across his back. Bug put the Hawken down and looked back at me. "He shot at you?"

I nodded.

"And missed?" Bug had a real yearning mixed in with his words, like a man with an itch he couldn't scratch. His eyes lit up like a mountain lion stalking a deer.

"I guess I got lucky," I told him.

"The Good Lord smiled on you, son," he said and glanced up to the sky before he turned back to the river, picked up his ax and chopped at the earth some more.

"Yes sir," I agreed. "I'm real grateful too." I knelt down beside him. "I brought you some pan bread and bacon. Are you hungry?"

"Bread?" His eyes jerked up from the river ford and bored into mine. They had the same look as Morton's eyes had the last time I saw him, a hungry man about to be fed. "I ain't had fresh bread in months," he muttered.

"Here you are, sir." I handed him the plate.

He tore off a big hunk and stuffed it into his mouth. His gaze flicked back to the river, a broad smile across his face.

7

The sun hadn't even snuck up over the snow-capped Sierra Nevada Mountains yet when I crawled out of my bedroll to stoke up the fire. I put on enough coffee, bacon and pan bread for everyone in camp. After the coffee brewed and with the last of the bread in the skillet, Bug Riddle pushed himself to his feet with his crutch, grabbed his rifle, limped to the fire and sat on a log beside me.

I gave him a cup of coffee and some breakfast. "Good morning, sir," I said, my tone full of eagerness. Today looked to be awful exciting. I had set my mind on finding K.O. Manuel and was raring to get at it, in spite of my promise to wait here for Eban.

Boyd soon joined us and took the food and coffee I offered with his usual wide grin. "This is a real treat for me Tom. I do all the cooking here and I ain't got the hang of flapjack bread yet, not by a long shot."

I smiled back. "You do real good with rabbits, Boyd."

"Sure I do. Rabbits are easy. I'll bag another one right after breakfast," he promised and waved his hand over the rifle leaning on the log beside him.

"When you've got that rabbit maybe you can ride down to Weber Creek with me?" I poured myself a cup of coffee.

"Mind you now, Tom, I don't want you misunderstanding me none. I'd like to help you find this feller what's causing such a ballyhoo around here, but I can get at least one wagon loaded down at the saw mill before your friend Eban shows back up. Pa and me, well, we really need the money."

I frowned but Boyd had a point. "You're right. I can't ask you to help me rustle up a fellow as dangerous as K.O. Manuel for free, and I can't pay what it's worth. I'll go myself." A shiver ran up my backbone as I walked over to Rojo, fully intending to saddle him and ride out alone. Looking for K.O. Manuel seemed scarier than I'd first thought it would be.

"Would you consider the help of a shot-up old army major, son?"

"What?" I spun to the sound. "Major Lawson, are you up to something like this, sir?" I asked with a bit of wonder. Yesterday the Major had barely been able to ride.

"Well, I might have to take it slow," he admitted. "But if I could get some of that coffee and bread I'd like to try. I'll need a horse though." He sat up without any help. His face had lost most of the pastiness and even had a bit of color about it. "Will you give me a hand over to the fire, son?"

"Sure, sir. I'll help you." And I gave him a tug up to his feet.

He braced a hand on my shoulder and took one shaky step after another. He groaned each time he moved the wounded leg, but he kept at it until he reached the fire.

After the Major sat down on the log, Bug Riddle pushed himself up with his crutch and picked up his Hawken rifle. "You can ride my mustang paint, Major. She's a bit skittish round strangers but if you handle her gentle she'll warm up to you."

"Thank you, Mr. Riddle. That's kind of you," said the Major.

"Her name's Lola. I reckon she could use the exercise," Bug called over his shoulder as he hobbled off toward the ravine.

Boyd picked up his rifle and stood. "I hope you find that feller you're looking for, Tom. Thanks for the breakfast." He tipped his hat to the Major and strode off through the pines.

Major Lawson took the coffee and the plate of food with a nod of thanks. He sipped the coffee, sat the cup down and picked up the bread. "Son, you've put a lot into finding me and Lord knows I'm grateful to you, but I would be mighty pleased if you could tell me the whole story of how you came here, starting with when you met my daughter, while I'm busy with this fine meal."

I nodded, glad for the opportunity to tell the Major all I knew about the scoundrels at the mining cooperative and the downright wickedness of K.O. Manuel. So I started back on Friday when Lacey showed up at the cafe. Throughout the whole rundown Major Lawson only asked a few questions and mostly sat and ate his breakfast. I finally worked my way up to Boyd leading us to the spot where we'd found him. Then I moved on to the idea I'd gotten from Jeremiah Wiggins that K.O. Manuel camped along Weber Creek north of the ford, and how I planned on going there this morning.

"Anyhow, that's the long and short of it, sir. I'd bet K.O. already left his campsite to do whatever evil deed needs doing today, so it ought to be safe for us."

The Major downed the last of his coffee. "I'm impressed, Tom. You've put a lot of thought into this and figured things out real well. I'll go with you to find this campsite, but only because it seems like the best and fastest way to protect both you and my daughter from this monster. I have no doubt he'll kill you if he can and, if he ever finds out who Lacey is and where she's staying, heaven only knows what might happen to her. But you must do exactly what I tell you. Is that clear?"

I knew the Major was right. "Okay, sir, I'll do what you say."

"Good, now let's see if I can make friends with Lola." He swabbed the last chunk of bread through the bacon grease at the bottom of his plate then quickly polished it off. "Let me try walking to Lola by myself, but I would be grateful if you'd bring my saddle over."

"Yes, sir," I said, wondering if I should help him to his feet.

Major Lawson struggled some but he stood up by himself, and with a broad grin slowly limped off to the west of the pines where the horses were tethered. He still groaned each time he moved the bad leg but it was clear he could make it without my help. Bug Riddle's paint snorted and pulled back on her rein when he got near, but he talked to her nice and soft and soon she let him stroke her neck. In no time she nuzzled him with her big snout.

I hurried over with all of the riding gear but when I got close Lola shied away again.

Major Lawson held out his hand to stop me. "Here, let me have that tack, Tom." Once he'd grabbed hold of it he started talking to Lola again and soon he had the mare saddled and ready to ride. Major Lawson had a nice way with horses, I thought.

I followed him down the slope toward the river. As we passed Bug I waved and he nodded a closemouthed goodbye. He wasn't hacking the earth with the ax now. Instead, he sat with the Hawken cradled in his lap, waiting for K.O. to cross the river and into his gun sight. Then, I was sure, Bug would blow that red shirted devil to kingdom come.

Only a few people wandered along the street as we rode through Coloma. The shops had just opened and Web Lawson eyed each store we came to. He took special notice of P.T. Burns General Merchandise where the roll up pants still hung in the window, and turned to me. "I could use some new clothes. Mine are rotten and full of the stink of my dead horse. Maybe on our way back we can stop here."

I gulped and pointed to the Golden Nugget. "You can, sir, but once I worked at that saloon, cleaning up in the mornings. The mining cooperative office is next door. A lot of folks here still know me, even in this Mexican hat. Word might get back to K.O. right quick if somebody spotted me."

The Major's gaze quickly found the small sign hanging in front of the staircase beside the saloon. "So they do their recruiting in the bar, do they?"

"Yes sir, at least that's what I think."

Major Lawson grimaced. "I need to find this guy soon. There is too big a chance that someone I care about will get hurt if I don't."

"I'm kind of worried about Lacey too, sir."

He looked over at me, eyebrows raised. "Yes, I'm worried about Lacey, but it sounds like she's safe for the present. Right now you're the one that's in real danger."

I nearly gagged. The idea that I could get hurt, maybe even killed, kept slapping me in the face. Yet no matter how many times it did I still wanted to chase the trouble I knew was coming. It was hard to understand, but I craved the excitement all the danger caused. It tingled up and down my backbone, thrilling me from the top of my head to the tips of my toes. Somehow I loved it, even though it scared me to death at the same time.

Still, I kept my head down, my face hidden behind the broad brim of the sombrero, until we were well beyond the last building in town. There the stands of pines grew thick. The river could only be seen through an occasional gap in the forest, but the murmur of rushing water rippled between the trees clear enough.

A flurry of wings burst from the grass near the trail. The vultures in the grove flashed in my mind. I ripped the shotgun from its scabbard, cocked it, and had it up to my shoulder, ready to fire, in the blink of an eye. My heart pounded. Sweat beaded on my forehead. But I didn't shoot. "Quail," I gasped, realizing how tense I was as the last of the plump, gray, low flying birds disappeared among the trees. From my right I heard the Major chuckle and turned to face him, sure my face was as red as a ripe apple.

The Major smiled. He didn't look like he thought my being fooled should embarrass me. "You sure got that heavy shotgun up and ready real quick," he said with an encouraging tone. "But you held your fire when you realized it was only a covey of quail. Some men would have shot as soon as the gun was at their shoulder. If you'd hit a bird or two that wouldn't be so bad, but suppose it had been an innocent stranger who startled you and you killed him without thinking. That would've been terrible."

The Major's praise lifted my spirits a bit. I really wanted Lacey's pa to like me. "Well," I started talking kind of slow, unsure if what I had to say would impress him or not. "I thank you, sir, but to tell the truth I'm not out and out clear I can shoot a man. I've never been much for killing anything. I don't like seeing critters suffer," I admitted, knowing full well I was talking to an army man whose business was shooting people. I hoped he wouldn't think less of me because of how I felt.

"That's the way all right thinking men are, son," the Major replied. "Killing an animal for food is necessary, and sometimes a man has to kill another man in self-defense. Still, it's a hard thing to do."

"But you're in the army and the army is supposed to kill people," I blurted.

Major Lawson shrugged. "There are men in the army who actually enjoy killing. That's true. But they aren't good men and they are often trouble for their commanders. There's a lot of brave talk about fights, battles and heroism—men will be men—but when push comes to shove most soldiers would rather not fight if there's any reasonable alternative. War is, after all, dirty, hard and very dangerous."

I nodded. "I never thought of it that way, sir."

"We're hunting a man now, Tom, just like we would hunt a deer," the Major went on. "When we find him it's likely that there will be gunplay and someone, hopefully the man we're looking for and not one of us, will be killed. I've noticed how thoughtful you can be. In spite of what you just told me, I have to believe you've spent a lot of time considering whether you'll be willing to pull the trigger when and if the time comes."

I looked down at the shotgun resting in my arm. "Yes sir, I reckon I thought about it some," I said softly, almost in a whisper. My mind tore back to the night before I went after Jeremiah and how I'd determined that if it came down to it I'd shoot him because it was better than being shot. The Major was right. The same things mattered here. Deep down I really didn't want to shoot another man, but if I had to do it I would. I'd set my mind on it.

I released the hammer so the shotgun wouldn't go off accidentally but left it cradled in my arm, ready to use if needed. Then I turned back to the Major, who stared at me with a stern face and calm eyes, waiting, I knew, for the answer to a question that had never been asked. "I'm ready, sir," I said in a strong, clear voice.

The Major broke a small smile, not one of happiness or frolic but one of satisfaction that I'd given him the answer he expected. He nodded like he had known all along, and nudged Lola to a trot. "Let's find this scoundrel's camp," he called.

At the ford on Weber Creek we stopped. Major Lawson turned to me. "So this Jeremiah boy said K.O. Manuel is camped somewhere off to our right," he said in a matter of fact way, but it was really more of a question.

Right here in the middle of the stream, where the current is fast and the water deep, Sadie, the mare I rode when I first came to the gold country, stepped into a pothole and threw me head over heels into the creek. I'd been washed downstream and nearly drowned before I got lucky enough to grab onto one of Sadie's stirrups and pull my head back above the water. I quickly pushed the memories away. The Major wanted an answer. "Yes sir," I said smartly. "That's what Jeremiah told me yesterday."

Still I felt queasy. The old terror I once had from coming so close to drowning that day suddenly ran up my back. Maybe Lacey's pa could see it in my face. He wore the same stern, cold-eyed look that he'd had back when we talked about shooting people. He seemed awful aware of little things like that, and real concerned that I agreed to whatever we were about to do. It seemed like he looked after me kind of like Pa had done before he died.

No doubt I felt better with the Major here so I kicked Rojo's flank and waded into the water, facing my trembling nerves and the memories at the same time. "Just past that big rock there's a good place to camp." I yelled over the rush of the stream. "Maybe that's where he is."

"Take it slow, Tom, and be careful," the Major called out. I heard Lola splash into the creek behind me.

I took Rojo around the rock. On the far side I saw the place where I'd come out of the water that day. After my family caught up with me we'd camped just beyond a thick stand of brush. It would be a great place for a killer to stay, out of sight from both the trail and the creek but still close to both. I guided Rojo up on the grassy space alongside the stream and waited for the Major catch up. "There's a campsite behind the bushes, sir," I pointed out when he pulled Bug Riddle's paint to a halt next to me.

"Do you know this area well, Tom?"

"A little, sir, I camped here a year ago."

"All right, you wait for me. I'll go over and see what's there now."

"Yes, sir." I knew as soon as I'd said it that I didn't want to sit and let the Major go alone into what could be K.O. Manuel's camp. I wanted to go too, but I'd promised to do what Major Lawson told me and so I'd wait as ordered. Still, while the Major rode slowly toward the brush, I pulled back the hammer on one barrel of the shotgun and eased my finger near the trigger, just in case trouble happened.

The Major pulled out his Paterson Colt and nudged Lola through the shrubs. Soon I couldn't see him anymore. My meddlesomeness got the best of me. I had to know what happened on the other side of those bushes. I edged Rojo toward the brush.

Major Lawson called me, calmly like there wasn't any hurry, but I busted into the campsite as fast as I could. The place where I'd stayed after almost drowning in the creek looked like a lot more people used it over the last year. Someone had built a real nice fire pit and moved some logs around it to sit on, but I saw no sign that anyone camped here now.

The Major squatted beside the dead fire, fingering a handful of ashes. "If our friend was here he's been gone for a couple of days at least, probably longer." He pitched the cold cinders back and stood. "Then again, maybe he's camped somewhere else close by. Do you know of more campsites around?"

I grinned. An officer in the American army asked my opinion about where a real bad man he'd been sent to nab might be holed up. I pulled myself up proud and pointed downstream. "There are probably more spots further on," I said. "When I was here a year ago folks were mining in the shallows where the water eddies near the American River."

"Why don't we ride down there then," the Major said and climbed on Lola.

We picked our way through the rocks, trees and brush beside the Weber Creek. Near the American River three Mexicans worked a rocker, a shorter version of the sluice the Chinamen had used. One man pitched ore into a hopper, another one poured water onto the ore to wash it across cleats nailed on the bottom to catch the gold, while the last man rocked the whole contraption like a baby's cradle to make things flow easy.

"Morning," Major Lawson began. "Finding any color?"

The men looked up with fear in their eyes. The rocker man turned to answer. "Someone has mined this place before us, Senor," he said. "There is only a little gold left."

"Have you been here long?" the Major went on. The man who poured the water took a step back and slid one hand down closer to a pistol tucked into his waistband. The Major must have noticed but he kept talking in a calm voice. "We're looking for someone we heard might be camped close to here. I thought maybe you'd seen him. He rides a pinto and wears a dirty white straw hat and a red shirt. We think he killed some miners upstream a while back."

The faces of the three miners relaxed when they heard this news. The rocker man nodded. "Si, we see this man, Senor, a week ago, maybe two. He say we must leave. Someone else need to mine our claim. He carry a shotgun like you." He pointed at me. "The man speak my language and say he will shoot if we do not go, but he no see Jose behind him with the rifle." He flicked a finger toward the woods. A man in a wide sombrero stepped from behind a tree and cocked a heavy flintlock aimed at the Major's back.

Lacey's Pa didn't even look, just tipped his hat as calm as could be. "Vaya con Dios," he said in Mexican, turned Lola and rode back upstream.

I followed him, my mind in a whirl. K.O. Manuel had tried to run those Mexicans off their claim and it's likely he'd run the Chinamen on Hangtown Creek off theirs. He'd shot the two men up Weber Creek in the back and beat another one to death. Now he'd found a new place to camp and that would make him a lot harder to find. He could be anywhere. But deep down I knew that if K.O. really wanted to kill me he'd still be close.

##

As we neared Coloma Major Lawson began to sway from side to side in his saddle. When he went so far to his left that I thought he would fall I called out, my voice loud in case he'd fallen asleep or something. "Sir, are you all right?"

"Oh," he moaned. "I'm afraid I pushed myself too far, Tom."

"Would you like to stop?" I asked.

"No, not yet, maybe in town. I thought I saw a barbershop when we rode through. Do they have a place to take a hot bath?"

I couldn't help a small chuckle. Major Lawson was in better shape than I'd thought. "There's one a little ways past the Golden Nugget, right across the road from P.T. Burns store."

"That would be perfect. Maybe after a hot bath, a haircut and a shave I'll feel like a civilized man again."

"Civilized, sir?" To me, civilized folks were like Eban or Doak Wiggins, men who didn't do bad stuff and would help others when they could. It was the new miners, fresh off the boat from the east, dressed in fancy clothes, hair cut neat, always shaved and bathed, who caused most of the trouble around here lately, them and folks like K.O. Manuel and the others at the mining cooperative.

Now the Major let out a small laugh. "You've never been to a big city back east, have you Tom?" He still wobbled a bit as he rode but he'd grabbed onto the saddle with one hand and that steadied him some.

"No sir. I've been here in California most of my life, lived on a farm in the Santa Clara Valley south of San Francisco up till last year."

"It's a different world back there. Lacey and I were in Washington before we came here. It's a bustling, important place. Senators and Congressmen ride around in fancy carriages and dine in expensive restaurants with beautiful, well-dressed women. There are hundreds of shops that sell everything you can think of, even things imported from far off places like India and China."

"Holy Moses, India and China! I read some stories about them in McGuffey's Reader and I think I saw some Chinamen on Hangtown Creek yesterday. They were gone this morning and some new guys mined there. I wondered if maybe K.O. ran them off."

The Major stared hard at me, a no-nonsense look on his face. "Yeah, you might be right, Tom. That seems to be how the cooperative gets claims. They scare away miners who don't speak English, mostly Mexicans, but now that boatloads of Chinese are coming into San Francisco the mining cooperative will target them too. Things are growing so fast everywhere in California that it's hard to control lawbreakers."

"Why do people come to San Francisco, sir? There's no gold there."

"Because it has such a good port."

"But, sir, San Francisco ain't even as big as Coloma."

"You haven't seen San Francisco in a while. A year ago it was a sleepy Mexican village. Now you wouldn't recognize it. It must be ten times as big as back then, and still people live in tents all around town. And it will continue to grow. Everyday ships show up from all over the world, loaded with men wanting gold. The word is that many thousands more are on their way."

"Thousands?" I blurted. The miners along Hangtown Creek already complained about all the new men who came here from somewhere else and didn't know the first thing about mining, much less how to survive in the rugged gold country. The idea that thousands more were coming was downright scary. It was a number that sounded so big I couldn't get a firm grip on how many people it really meant.

"Many thousands, Tom." The Major had a smile now, clearly enjoying the wonderment he'd caused me by tossing around numbers so farfetched. "It takes a ship about the same time to get here from the east as it does a wagon but a wagon can only go in the summer. The ships started arriving this spring but it will take until fall for those who come overland. There could be as many as one hundred thousand people who will to come to California this year alone. Some of them will even be from Europe and Africa."

"Wow, that's a lot to think about, sir," I muttered, bothered how all these new men would fit in. Already more miners got robbed or killed than a year ago.

"California is going to change fast. It already has." Major Lawson let loose his grip on the saddle and swept his hand towards the town of Coloma down the road in front of us. "Look how this town has grown. When James Marshall started building the saw mill here this was nothing but wilderness. Now, only a year after the news of gold got out, the whole country is teeming with people. You've seen that for yourself I expect."

"Yes sir, I reckon I have seen some of it," I admitted, but I had to wonder why the Major talked like he thought more new men here would be good. When we got to the first buildings in town I ducked down, my face tucked in behind the wide brim of the sombrero. We passed the saw mill and I dared a peek into the lot but didn't see Eban or the freight wagon. Judging by the sun it was still too early for him. I kept my head low, and we rode by the Golden Nugget Saloon. The Major stopped in front of the Tyler Wright Tonsorial Parlor.

"Will you be okay getting back to Bug Riddle's campsite, Tom?" He carefully slid off Lola and landed on his good leg.

"Yes sir. I expect so." I gave a quick glance back toward the saloon.

"I'll see you there," he said, and limped over to the barber's door.

I sat on Rojo to mull things over. What I really wanted to do now was talk to Eban, but for that I'd have to ride up the Hangtown Road. And I had a real bad feeling that K.O. Manuel might just sit somewhere up there waiting to shoot me when I came along.

Out of the corner of my eye I saw a fellow ride by me on a mule. I couldn't help but turn to stare. The rider, who looked a lot like Jeremiah with stringy brown hair under a beat up slouch hat, had on raggedy, homemade pants with a pair of fancy, hand tooled Mexican riding boots sticking out of the bottom. If this fellow didn't work for K.O. Manuel I'd eat my straw sombrero. He might be on his way to meet the killer right now.

I took out after him nice and slow; face down behind the hat brim, looking like I hadn't a care in the world and no curiousness at all about the fellow on the mule ahead of me. Still my heart pounded like the blacksmith's hammer and sweat gushed from my forehead like a waterfall on a Sierra stream. But it didn't seem like the guy on the mule had noticed me—at least he hadn't looked back.

We neared the eastern edge of town. I slowed Rojo some. If the guy I followed worked with K.O. Manuel and headed to K.O.'s new campsite right now, I'd be willing to bet my brand new roll-up pants against the raggedy ones Mule Boy had on that he would turn up the road that went to Hangtown. When he did he'd likely look back towards town like most men would to see if anybody came along after him. He'd see me for sure. If I stayed this close to him on the trail it might make him edgy, and that worried me.

But I kept after him, head down behind the hat brim, eyes glued to the dirt below. And that's when I noticed the hoof prints the mule left. Three of the shoes looked the same as any of the hundreds of other prints splattered across the dusty street, but one, from the right foreleg, always left a small pile of dirt midway down the outside where one of the nails worked loose.

If I hadn't been so dead set on hiding my face I'd never have noticed, but now each little pile of dirt seemed to leap up off the ground and swat me in the nose. I knew I could follow the mule almost anywhere he went and that meant I didn't have to be so close and take the chance of the rider fretting over who I might be.

I pulled Rojo to a halt, hopped to the ground, led the chestnut over to the side of the road and started in on tightening his cinches. Every so often I'd sneak a peek over the saddle and only show a small part of my face. In no time, like I'd figured, the guy took a hard gander back towards town when he turned up the road to Hangtown.

I could see Mexican water bags hanging across the saddle. Could he be bringing water to K.O.? That's one more bet I'd be willing to make.

After he rode out of sight I leapt back on Rojo and moseyed along behind him, sure I could spot where the little piles of dirt kicked up by the loose nail left the trail. I was double certain that they would lead me to K. O. Manuel's new camp.

I turned up the road to Hangtown Creek. Past the towering redwood trees to the west and the lowland filled with pines on the east, the road twisted and turned. It rose steadily from the river valley until, on both sides of the trail, oaks replaced the evergreens and it smoothed out some with the turns easier than those closer to Coloma.

Soon I'd made it halfway to the top of the hill. Somewhere up ahead Mule Boy rode on, but I still couldn't see him and hadn't since town. That had to be good, I thought. He likely didn't even know about me dogging his tracks.

Then a woman screamed. The loud clatter of hoof beats came from up ahead. Someone came this way fast. I ducked into the oaks east of the road and hid, fretful it might be K.O. When I got Rojo turned back toward the trail a buggy showed up, pulled by a fine, black stallion running full out down the hill, a dark haired lady in a fancy hat pulling back on the reins for all she was worth, yelling at the top of her lungs for the horse to stop.

A runaway buggy! Sure as water runs downhill the woman would get hurt bad if she didn't get some help quick. I knew I ought to save her bacon, but if I went after her I'd likely lose track of the mule, its rider, and maybe my only chance to find K.O. Manuel.

Still, somebody had to chase that buggy down and stop it.

I started to walk Rojo out of the woods but I heard another horse coming fast. Maybe they would save the woman. I held up and a mustang like the one Joshua rode sped by me carrying a Mexican fellow. Now I started to fret. The Mexican wore a straw sombrero like the one I had on, but looked way shorter and a lot stockier than Joshua. Yet the mustang seemed a spitting image of Joshua's horse.

Back on the trail I spun Rojo first toward Coloma then toward Hangtown Creek. Should I follow the Mexican chasing the buggy or keep after the mule and find K.O.'s camp? Holy Moses, maybe the Mexican fellow stole Joshua's horse, maybe he's K.O, maybe he'd been to the cabin, where he hurt Maggie, Eban or Joshua—or even Lacey!

I swallowed hard, took a deep breath and blew it out with a wheeze. I didn't have much time but I had to think this thing through. First off, I knew K.O. would have a hard time getting past Joshua and Eban both. He could do it, sure, but if I had to bet on it, I wouldn't bet on K.O. Maybe the mustang only looked like Joshua's. No way could I tell that for certain so I'dkeep after the mule. That's what Eban would do and that's what my gut told me to do.

With my mind set again on finding K.O, I commenced scouting around for the telltale hoof print with the pile of dirt from the loose nail but nowhere on the road could I find one. Two horses and an out of control buggy had splattered dirt clods, dust, more hoof prints and wheel marks all across the mule's trail. Dang, I thought, what do I do now? Maybe there would be more little piles up the road.

I nudged Rojo and went on, scouring the trail from one side to the other, but the piles of dirt that only a short time ago had stood out like the tallest mountain in the Sierra had vanished. Surely somewhere along the road one hoof print with the loose nail would show up. After all, every one of them couldn't have been covered over. But no matter how hard I searched I didn't find one single print from the mule.

Finally I raised my face to the sky and silently pled for the help Doak Wiggins said might come my way. Then I smiled, feeling better all of a sudden. I gave Rojo a kick and trotted up the hill, knowing full well I could be riding headlong into trouble. Around the next curve I slowed again and once more searched high and low for any sign of the unmistakable track of the mule. I still couldn't find a one.

While I pondered what to do next a muleskinner yelled like he needed to get his team to work together. I didn't recognize the voice right off but knew it wasn't Eban. Staying heedful of the danger I faced, I ducked back into the trees once more and hid behind a bramble in a small clearing among the oaks.

In no time one of our freight wagons rolled by. I recognized the mules, but Woody Dunn drove them, not Eban. I hadn't seen Woody since he told me I had to tend the cafe 'cause of Maggie's baby coming. But Eban had promised to be back today. Something happened, something bad. I knew it. I needed to catch up with Woody to find out.

But before I could get Rojo going I heard a thud, followed right off by a grunt, from somewhere up the hill. Quickly another thud came and the long, loud moan of a man who'd been hurt bad rumbled through the woods. Could it be K.O. beating up on Mule Boy? I leaned over and hugged Rojo's neck to keep the chestnut quiet. But mostly I needed something to hold on to, something to keep my hands from shaking so.

"Stupid gringo! I kill you someday." The voice came from not far up the road, no more than fifty paces away, I'd guess. My whole body shook.

"I'm sorry, my Pa needed me," somebody else whined.

"Bah, now I miss the wagon because you sleep late. Then you lie to me like all gringos do." Another sound came, sharp like a face slap, answered by a blubbering yelp.

"It won't happen again, never. I swear. Let me be. Please, let me be," sobbed the other guy, whimpering, begging. I started to understand Jeremiah now. He must have gone through the same thing. Silently I thanked God that Jeremiah had seen the light along the road that day and refused to shoot me. Otherwise I knew I'd be a goner already.

"Do all gringos cry like a woman? Cross me again I kill you. Vamoose." K.O. yelled loud, his tone snotty and oozing with high-handedness.

"Yes sir. Yes sir. Right away, sir."

The sudden silence chilled me. I held tight to Rojo, shaking, scared out of my gourd. I heard the mule lumbering this way, picking up speed as fast as a beat up old jackass could. Soon I saw them, the boy swatting the jenny with the end of the reins. Except for a thick streak of blood that ran down the side of his mouth his face looked as pale as a freshly whitewashed wall. I turned back toward where I'd heard K.O.'s voice. The drum of the mule's hoof beats faded behind me.

I let go of Rojo's neck and slipped the shotgun out. If K.O. knew I hid here there would be hell to pay. My chest heaved, my hands shook and my heart pounded hard. I sat up tall in Rojo's saddle and quietly cocked one hammer of the scattergun. If K.O. showed his ugly face I'd blow the rotten polecat straight into the next world.

"Andele!" Hoof beats thundered from up the road again, this time heading toward the top of the hill. I rushed to the edge of the trail in time to see K.O. and the pinto wheel around the next curve and out of sight. I had half a mind to take after him but thought better of it. I knew where to find him now. I'd be back tomorrow. Besides, I needed to look into the runaway buggy, the Mexican guy and why Woody Dunn drove the freight wagon instead of Eban. I turned Rojo toward Coloma.

When I got nearer to town, with the redwoods tall to my left and the pines thick on my right, I saw the buggy sitting by the side of the road ahead at the far end of a straight stretch. The Mexican fellow and the woman stood behind it talking while the mustang munched grass nearby. She looked like somebody real important, with a fancy dress that only a queen from some place far away would wear and a hat with a green feather so long that every Injun west of the Mississippi would take a fancy to it.

At least the fellow had saved her, and he couldn't be K.O. Still, to be safe, I pulled Maggie's little gun from my pocket and stuck it in the waistband of my roll-up pants at the small of my back. The woman looked up and stared straight at me. She said something to the Mexican guy who right away walked her over and helped her into the buggy seat. The reins popped and she rattled off toward Coloma.

But now the Mexican fellow stared at me. I started to sweat again and thought about pulling out the shotgun, but if I did the guy might think I aimed on shooting him and might shoot first. When the guy turned the mustang sideways and climbed on I couldn't help but think how the horse sure did look exactly like Joshua's. My left hand started to shake, my palms clammy. But I kept my eyes on the Mexican guy, ready for anything.

The man ripped off his sombrero and spread his arms wide. "Tom," he shouted.

My jaw dropped flat to ground. It all came out of the blue, the one thing I never expected. "Eban." I yelled back and kicked Rojo to a gallop, my heart thumping again. I hurried to meet my friend. When I got close my excitement spewed over. I had way too much to say. "I followed a guy from town," I hollered. "He rode a mule and wore fancy boots—"

"Hold on, Tom," Eban interrupted his hand up, palm forward.

I yanked back on the reins and pulled Rojo to a stop. "Anyway," I went on, "he led me to K.O.'s new camp and after that K.O. beat him—"

"Now wait up, son." This time Eban held up both palms. "You're talking so fast I can't hear it all with these old ears. I ain't never seen you so riled up about anything. Let's you and me ride on toward Coloma and then you can tell me the whole thing real slow, starting from the beginning."

"Okay, Eban." I grabbed a deep breath and started in on my story again slow and easy. By the time we reached the river I'd managed to get him caught up on everything that had happened since yesterday. "Anyway, that's about it," I said. "But who was that lady in the buggy? I never seen a woman dressed as grand as her, like a famous lady in a book."

"That, my young friend, was Miss Dancy Bellotti, and she sings down at the Golden Nugget every night but Sunday. Ain't she something?" Eban's eyes had a dreamy, faraway look and I could understand why. But Dancy Bellotti, decked out in her fancy dress and hat and the most eye-catching female I'd ever seen by a long shot, didn't hold a candle to Lacey's prettiness.

But in spite of how all Miss Bellotti's fancy clothes nearly caused my heart to jump out of my chest I still had questions for Eban. "So why are you wearing that sombrero and riding Joshua's horse? Why is Woody Dunn driving the wagon? Did something happen back home?"

Eban looked down at the ground and wrung his hands together. Finally he shook his head and turned back to me. "I didn't know if I should tell you this or not, son, but I reckon I got to. That K.O. feller came by the cafe yesterday, asking after you. Maggie talked to him. He liked to have scared her to death. He's got a way about him, a real mean way. Maggie don't get rattled easy. She's seen her share of bad men."

"Lacey!" I sputtered. "Was he looking for her at all? Is she all right?"

"Maggie shut down the cafe." Eban went on. "Both her and Lacey are awful worried over you, but otherwise they're fine. They're at the cabin with Joshua where they'll be safe. He won't let anybody in, plus we sent word for help from Sacramento City. I'll talk to Wimmer as soon as I get to the saw mill, let him know what's going on. I expect he can rustle up some more men. We got to find this feller fast or a lot more folks are liable to get killed."

"What about you, Eban," I asked. "You're riding Joshua's horse. You got on a different shirt and you're wearing a sombrero like me. K.O. asked about you, didn't he?"

Eban's lip curled into a snarl. "Well, sorta." He spit in the dust. "He asked Maggie where the useless gray haired old mossback that drove the wagon was. When Maggie told him she didn't know anybody like that she said he gave her a look Lucifer himself would've been proud of. Told her he'd find me anyhow, whether she said anything or not."

My eyes narrowed and I could feel the skin on my forehead burn. Now I'd put everybody I cared about in danger, not just Lacey but Maggie, Eban, and Joshua too. Waiting for help would take way too long. This was my fault. I had to make dang sure nobody got hurt. Tomorrow morning, early, I would take care of K.O. Manuel once and for all. I set my mind on it. I had to do it.

"Tom, you okay?" Eban asked, his voice loud.

"Oh." I jerked back from the scheme brewing in my mind. "I'm sorry, I guess I was thinking about Lacey and Maggie and all the trouble I caused." I said it so that Eban wouldn't stew over what I was cooking up.

"You ain't the cause of this, Tom," he went on, softer now. "It's all the doing of that K.O. feller and his henchmen. Bad men make trouble for the good folks in the world. That's the way it's always been. You best get used to it."

"Yeah, but if I hadn't gone looking for Lacey's pa we'd be safe now," I said.

"That's true, but you still done right. If you hadn't gone after the Major he might've died. Sometimes bad things happen to folks who do good. This is one of those times. Now we got to stay calm, stay together and take care of things," he said with some fire, then took a deep breath and added. "Good always wins out over bad in the end."

I looked straight at him. He had a sure as shooting look that made me feel better right off. How K.O. Manuel could ever call Eban a useless old mossback I couldn't understand.

"Thanks, Eban. You always find a way to ease my mind when trouble comes." I smiled in spite of how scary things seemed. I felt some better now that Eban had gotten back here, but the news that K.O. had been to the cafe unsettled me something fierce—all the more reason to take care of K.O. Manuel as soon as I could.

Where the road took a hard left turn into Coloma we stopped. To the right a narrow trail led to the ford across the American River. Eban pointed that way. "You go back to Bug Riddle's place and wait. Stay out of sight and out of trouble. I got things to do at the saw mill. I'll be as quick as I can. And I'll find the Major and bring him with me. Now it ain't that I don't trust you but you've been way too headstrong lately. I want your word of honor you'll go straight to the camp and stay there."

I nodded. "I'll go," I said honestly, the promise easy to keep. I didn't plan on going after K.O. until tomorrow morning anyway. While I headed to the ford I knew Eban would keep his eye on me as long as he possibly could just to make sure I did like he asked. I didn't even need to look back to check.

He'd said I'd been headstrong lately and I reckoned I had, but I'd rather look at what I'd done more as something any good man would've done. Still, I knew Maggie and Lacey would figure that my following the boy on the mule had been out and out foolhardy. When it came down to it most folks would agree with them. And the risk in what I planned for tomorrow I couldn't deny, that's for sure. I could get hurt real easy, but I had to do it for Lacey and Maggie, for everybody really.

At the ford I stopped and peered up the hill on the far side of the river. I could barely make out Bug Riddle at the top of the ravine, staring down at me with the Hawken rifle in his left hand. I took off the sombrero and waved it. I didn't want to take any chance that Bug would mistake me for somebody else and decide to shoot.

But Bug put the rifle down and I splashed into the water. Midstream, with the rushing current churning around me, it suddenly came to me how calm I felt about everything I'd planned to do tomorrow. After all, I'd made up my mind to kill a man, no ifs ands or buts about it, and I wasn't even nervous, not one bit, not even a shake, a tingle, a twitch, nothing—as cool as a cucumber. Yes sir, it'll all be as easy as peach cobbler. I didn't have a worry in the world. Not a one. Nope. No sweat.

After Rojo climbed onto the far bank, I wiped my forehead with the sleeve of my shirt. It seemed a lot hotter today than yesterday and right off I mopped my brow again, this time with the other arm. It must be about the hottest day ever around here I decided. On the way up the hill, I whistled a song I'd heard last summer at the beef stew feeds Maggie had on Sunday afternoons. Still, in spite of the heat, I felt good, real good. I wiped the sweat away again, still whistling, then dried my clammy palms on my roll-up pants, and wondered why my left hand suddenly shook so dang hard.

##

The sun set a little while ago and the sky over the American River slowly filled with stars. I'd made more pan bread and a pot of beans. Boyd bagged two rabbits that we'd roasted over the open fire. Eban and the Major got back from Coloma just before supper and Lacey's pa looked real dashing with his hair and beard trimmed nice and neat, and all dressed up in new blue pants, a gray shirt and a flat brimmed black hat. I figured they'd both spent most of the afternoon drumming up help in corralling K.O. Manuel and his cronies.

Boyd sat down next to Bug. I poured him a fresh cup of coffee then held the pot up high. "Anybody else want more?" I asked. When no one spoke up I put the pot beside the fire and sat next to the Major.

Eban hacked up a frog from his throat so everybody would listen to him. "You all know Major Lawson and me spent the afternoon with Wimmer and some other folks from Coloma. They've been concerned about the mining cooperative and the killings but didn't know a lot of what the Major does about these varmints. He turned a lot of heads there today but I'll let him tell you what he told them."

Major Lawson glanced around all of us till his eyes stopped on me. "I never thought bread and beans could taste so good, Tom." His eyes moved. "And Boyd, I'll always think of roast rabbit as a wonderful treat. I want to thank you, both of you, for feeding me so well in spite of such limited conditions. Mr. Riddle, I owe you a ton of thanks too for letting us impose on you like we've done. Your hospitality is appreciated."

Bug looked at the ground and mumbled under his breath.

The Major paused, twisted the tin cup in his hands and waited until Bug settled down. "Like Eban said, we talked to folks in town and tomorrow morning some men will go after the mining cooperative starting with its leader, Romano Manuel, or Romy as he's usually called." The Major used K.O.'s real first name. I hadn't known it. And he'd said K.O.'s last name not as 'Man-well' like the Mexicans would but as 'Man-u-well' like Americans did.

He took a sip of coffee before he went on. "Romy Manuel was born on a rancho near San Antonio to a wealthy Mexican of Spanish descent and an American woman from a well-to-do New Orleans family. When Texas declared its independence and Santa Ana marched on the Alamo there, his family fled to Mexico City for safety, but somewhere along the way bandits jumped them and killed his mother. Romy Manuel blamed her death on the Texicans. And to him there was no difference between Texicans and Americans. We were all gringos and equally responsible.

"By all accounts from people who knew him then, Manuel's mother had been a wonderful woman, warm and loving. He was her only child and she doted on him. Perhaps she spoiled him. But his father was a harsh man. He had a reputation for cruelty both in Mexico and Texas, and now Romy fell totally under his sway. Maybe this is where young Romy Manuel found the savagery he is so well-known for today, a simple case of like father like son."

"But Major," I blurted, "why do folks call him K.O?"

"That's a nickname Americans gave him from when he went across California fighting in cantinas. People paid a lot of money to see him pound another man senseless. They say he beat several men to death." Major Lawson stopped and looked at each one of us.

My left hand started to shake again. The same thing had happened off and on all day and I wondered if I was sick or something. I rested it on my leg and put my right hand on top. That seemed to help some.

Major Lawson started in again. "Romy Manuel was in San Diego when war broke out with Mexico. Reid Harrison and Frank Barney, once associates of mine on General Scott's staff in Washington and assigned similar supply duties in San Diego, sold Romy Manuel the information about Kearny's Army of the West's imminent arrival in California. Manuel knew the first piece of civilization Kearny would come to after a hard trek across a barren desert would be the rancho of a man named Walker, and Walker was married to Romy Manuel's cousin."

Now full dark and moonless and with only a pile of red-hot coals left of the fire, the faces of the men around me had faded into the shadows. Major Lawson grabbed a log in each hand and placed them one at a time on the embers. A strong flame flared up, flashing across the eyes of each of us.

I reached for the coffee pot. "Anybody want some?" I asked. "It's the last of it." Boyd and Eban both spoke out and I filled their cups before I poured the rest of the brew into mine.

When everyone settled down the Major continued. "We don't know exactly what happened, but we are fairly certain that Romy Manuel alerted someone in the local militia and they sent a company of lancers to intercept Kearny. They wound up at an Indian pueblo called San Pasqual close to the Walker Rancho. When Kearny found out he took his exhausted troops there at once. In the battle that followed the lancers killed over twenty men in Kearny's force of a little more than one hundred.

"But things got worse the next day when the lancers jumped Kearny again and chased his small, battered army up a hill. Only by the incredible bravery of Kit Carson and two other men who slipped through the lines and brought help from Stockton's naval force in San Diego did any of them live at all. Right about that time Harrison, Barney and Manuel disappeared and haven't been seen until now.

"As far as the government of the United States is concerned there is no hard evidence that any of the three did anything illegal during the war. While it looks very much like Harrison and Barney sold military secrets to the enemy there's no proof at all. And Romy Manuel, well, he was the enemy. But . . ." Major Lawson paused and looked hard at the face of each man one more time, " . . . we now have an eyewitness to what they've done here, if what I've heard is true, and that will be enough to convict them of murder, fraud and robbery. Tomorrow, God willing, we'll put an end to their evil doings."

"But sir," I exclaimed, "Lacey said K.O.—ah, I mean Romy Manuel—told General Santa Ana personally about Kearny's men. Ain't that the truth?"

The Major smiled and rolled his eyes back like folks do when they remember good times, then gave a little chuckle. "Lacey loved Santa Ana's name. You know how young girls can be. They latch onto things they like and make them bigger than they really are. I told her the story because everyone in San Francisco talked about it, and I also told her that Manuel's father and Santa Ana were lifelong friends. Romy Manuel was certainly a spy, but I doubt if he reported his discovery to Santa Ana personally."

What Lacey's pa said almost sounded like Lacey had fibbed some, and that ate at me a bit much. "But she said he told Santa Ana himself, and after the Americans were saved Santa Ana got mad and said he would kill K.O. and his cronies if he caught them."

"Well, Lacey got it almost right. Remember she was only twelve and a lot more interested in romantic notions than with the hard realities of war. She liked Santa Ana in spite of him being the enemy President because his name reminded her of Santa Claus. And she liked Kit Carson because he was brave and daring. Those are things that are important to young girls. But Santa Ana is a vengeful man, and he did order the execution of Romy Manuel and his accomplices after Kearny's men got away."

I rubbed my twitching left hand hard to calm it down. The Major made sense. Back during the war I know I wasn't as full grown as I am now. It stands to reason Lacey would be younger too. I'd just never thought of her as a little girl before. After all, she was real close to my age. I didn't know much about young girls and how they were, so I'd have to take the Major's word for it. Come to think of it, except for Lacey I didn't know much about girls at all, and she could be awful perplexing at times.

Eban stood. "We got a long day tomorrow. I think I'll turn in," he said.

Major Lawson held out his hand. "I agree. Will you help an old soldier to his feet, Eban?"

He pulled the Major up and he limped to his bedroll, using his army carbine for a crutch. Boyd helped his Pa to their bedrolls and it came to me how tired I was, so I turned in too.

In spite of the warm night I pulled the blanket tight around me. Somehow it felt comforting to have something to hide under out here in the open under the stars. A tiny chunk of the top of the moon crept over the Sierra to the west and a mockingbird chattered from the pines behind the hill. Lulled by the peace and quiet, my eyes fluttered shut. Sleep would come soon.

Right before I dozed off I heard it, coming from down by the river. Music! Someone strummed a guitar. Maybe it was the guy Bug almost shot yesterday. I settled back and listened. A man sang a wonderful tune in a high voice as smooth as Lacey's cheek. I could only get a word here and there 'cause he sang it all in Mexican, but somehow that didn't matter. The song had such a sad, mournful tone to it that I could imagine the words.

I closed my eyes and he told about his girl, Carmelita, a pretty dark haired senorita. He loved her very much. Then the song changed a little and another man sang along with the first one in an even higher voice. Strangely the two men together sounded so much sadder and lonelier than before. Something had happened to Carmelita, maybe she'd died, or maybe she went off with another man. Either way he missed her terribly.

The song made me think of Lacey. I'd known her for only a short time but right now I sure missed her a lot, like the fellow down by the river missed his senorita. I'd loved my Ma and now Maggie, but it didn't seem the same as Lacey. I couldn't get a solid grip around it but Lacey had a special hold on me. Like the singer and his Carmelita, I'd be powerful hurt if something happened to her. And that's why I had my mind so dead set on taking care of Romy Manuel tomorrow, once and for all.

He'd been lurking around the cafe yesterday. I knew if he ever figured out Webster Lawson had a daughter working there Lacey would be in more trouble than she could handle. I had to protect her from that. I couldn't count on the men from Coloma to do the job for me, even if the Major and Eban went with them. If you want something done right you do it yourself my Pa always said. I would take care of Romy Manuel in the morning, like I planned.

The song ended and a deep stillness rolled up from the river, but the sad, loneliness of the melody covered me like a thick fog. I turned onto my side and rubbed my twitching left hand. When I got back to the cabin I'd ask Maggie to look at it. She'd know what to do.

8

Rojo skidded to a stop in front of the cafe. I jumped to the ground and rushed through the open door. Inside the dining room chairs were tossed about, tables upended, broken dishes and crockery strewn across the floor. Morton sat off to the right at the only table still upright, his face splattered in a plate of mashed potatoes smothered in bloody gravy. Across the room Doak Wiggins leaned against the east wall, eyes blank, chest shredded from a shotgun blast. Jeremiah lay on the floor beside him, his face battered beyond belief, his teeth scattered among the chunks of busted plates.

In a heartbeat, as quick as a strong wind would blow a leaf, I swept into the kitchen. Eban lay face up just inside the door, a bullet hole between his eyes. Maggie slumped backwards across the kitchen table, the wooden handle of a butcher knife sticking up from her chest. I heard a gurgle from the corner. Baby Josie lay on the cot, her little feet and hands waving, while an arm wrapped around her waist held her tight against a yellow dress with blue flowers on it.

Lacey! Suddenly I was there, looking down from above onto a pool of blood that covered the cot, blood from Lacey's slashed throat.

"No!" I screamed. Lacey, Eban, Maggie gone. My eyes popped open. My breath came hard and fast. Sweat poured across my face. My left hand shook something terrible. Darkness covered the river. A thousand stars filled the sky. The moon hung pale and low off to the west. A faint glow from the coming sunrise tinted the eastern sky.

I moaned. It had been a dream, a horrible dream, a nightmare so real it jerked me clean out of a deep sleep. The out and out truth of what I had to do this very morning came crawling back over me slow and painful. I rubbed my tingling left hand and remembered. I had to kill the guy in the red shirt, Romy Manuel, before the dream, the horror I'd seen in my sleep, became real.

I flipped the blanket back, sat up, took a deep breath and tried to calm down. My heart pounded and my hand still shook, but the sun would rise soon enough so I might as well start some pan bread. There would be no more sleep for me tonight anyhow.

At the fire pit I looked at the ashes I'd banked up around the hot coals last night and thought back to how Major Lawson had checked the fire pit along Weber Creek yesterday to see how long it had been since anyone had camped there. I poked the embers around and blew on them. When I saw a red glow I tossed some small twigs and kindling on the coals. After I got a flame I laid several small logs on top. They turned black pretty quick then caught fire.

I couldn't help but recall what the Major told us last night about how Romy Manuel's own heart must have been charred black by hate after his mother got killed. I figured that's what caused the hot temper he carried with him now. Most folks can keep their temper under their hat. They are a lot like this small campfire. Because it is kept in check by the flat rock fire pit, it does a lot of good. It cooks the food we need to live, a lot like the stove at the cafe. But Red Shirt's hot-tempered heart beats wild. Like a burning cabin full of smoke and flame, Romy Manuel's hate destroys all the good things people work hard for, and leaves only cold, empty ashes behind.

The sky had brightened a lot by the time I finished with the last of the pan bread. The sun would peek over the mountains soon. I had fresh coffee brewing and a pot of leftover beans warming. I'd thrown in the last of the rabbit from yesterday just to give them a little extra kick.

Eban tossed around in his bedroll and sat up, stretched his arms to get rid of the kinks and pushed himself to his feet. He picked up his saddle, walked to the mustang, threw a blanket on his back, tossed the saddle on top and cinched it tight. He pulled his rifle out, checked the load and slid it back into the scabbard.

About that time Major Lawson sat up. "What a fine morning it is," he said and climbed to his feet without help.

Eban and the Major walked together over to the fire with Lacey's pa still leaning heavily on his carbine and limping. They both took the coffee I offered, each with a mumbled greeting and a half awake look pasted on his face.

When I handed over a tin plate of pan bread, bacon and beans their eyes brightened and hearty thanks came from each one. I smiled. I knew it meant they liked the food and were grateful I'd gotten up early to fix it. Somehow it meant a lot to me that people appreciated my cooking after all the guff I took when Maggie had baby Josie and I ran the cafe.

While I fixed up a plate for me, both of them ate without talking, their faces tight, worry clear in their wrinkled foreheads.

Lacey's pa held out his cup. "Warm this up for me, will you?" he asked.

"Sure, sir," I poured him more coffee.

"Thanks." He took a small sip and cleared his throat. "Son, you know what we plan on doing this morning," he said and sounded stuffy, like an officer giving orders to his men. "It's going to be dangerous, real dangerous. Eban and I talked this over yesterday and we both want you to stay here. There's too much chance that somebody will get hurt, maybe even killed, and we don't want that someone to be you."

"But sir—"

"No buts Tom," Eban interrupted. "I know you've done a lot and you're looking at bagging this scalawag like it's some sort of reward, but that ain't what it's likely to be. Romy Manuel's apt to fight to the death, kill as many men as he can, all out of pure spite. We can't go back and tell Maggie and Lacey you're dead. Right now you're a hero to the Major. You saved his life. That ain't bad for a boy just turned sixteen."

While Eban ran on about why I couldn't go hunting Romy Manuel, my mind flashed over the plan I'd made to shoot the four-flushing rattlesnake myself. I'd thought a lot about what I would do and how I'd do it, but I hadn't thought a whit about how I'd explain things to Eban. Now I realized that I only had to tell one big, fat lie and afterwards agree to whatever Eban and the Major told me and I'd be free do what I wanted as soon as they left. It'd be as easy as a Mexican siesta. After all, I'd gotten used to telling lies this week.

So I tossed the last bit of coffee in my cup onto the fire, setting off a loud hiss and a puff of steam. That ought to show them how mad I am. "That ain't fair," I yelled. "Just 'cause I'm sixteen don't make me a kid."

"No, Tom," the Major said in a tone that sounded more like a father talking to a son than the official army voice he'd used before. "Being sixteen simply means you have a lot of good years ahead of you. You are a remarkable young man and I owe you my life. I'd like to make sure you're around to help other men who get themselves in serious scrapes like I did. And after talking to Eban,

I'm pretty sure Lacey would never forgive me if I let something happen to you."

Major Lawson said some real nice things that I knew ought to make it easy for me to agree to stay behind. If only I could make both of them believe I would do what they said then I'd be scot-free to do whatever I wanted after they left. "Well," I grumbled while I put on my best woe is me look. "I guess I could stay here if you're going to make me."

"Promise me, son," Eban sounded determined.

"Oh . . ." I whined, and then I shrugged. "All right, Eban, I promise I won't go with you," I muttered, trying to seem as down in the dumps as I could.

"I don't want you to follow us after we leave. Give me your word," Eban added.

"Okay, I won't come after you," I mumbled, head still down and giving off the best hangdog look I could muster. After all, Eban had really only made me promise to not go after them when they left for town. He hadn't said a word about going after Romy Manuel by myself. This lying stuff was getting easier and easier the more I did it. Still, the lies didn't feel right. Maybe that's why my hand twitched so much right now.

"I'm glad you see it our way, Tom. It's for the best, someday you'll understand." Eban stood and turned to Lacey's pa. "Are you ready, sir?"

Major Lawson sighed. "As ready as I can be." Together they made their way to the horses, Lacey's pa still limping bad but not leaning on his carbine anymore.

They passed Boyd, with Bug scuffling along behind, about the same time a flood of sunlight surged down the river valley, washing out the predawn shadows in a blaze of color. Facing directly east, Boyd shielded his eyes with his hand, then sat down across the fire from me and held out a tin cup. "Morning, Tom," he said.

"Morning." I poured him coffee.

Bug struggled onto the log next to Boyd and muttered a couple of blurry, fuzzy words that I took as a hello.

I got them both food and picked up the plate I'd fixed earlier for myself. Together we ate quiet-like, listening to the small wrens and bush tits chirp from the pines while a red-tailed hawk let out a shrill screech every so often as it floated slowly overhead in search of its own breakfast.

I looked up when I heard the clomp of horses coming. Eban and the Major stopped near the fire. "We'll be back as soon as we can, Tom," Eban said. "Remember, you gave me your word you won't follow us." He wore a stern do-as-I-tell-you look.

I frowned. "I won't follow you, Eban," I promised, happy I could honestly agree. I knew now I could go after Romy Manuel as soon as they left. By the time the posse from Coloma caught up to me, Romy Manuel would be dead.

Still, Eban didn't look satisfied. "I can count on you, can't I?" he asked with one eyebrow raised.

I tried to put on my best don't worry about me smile. "I promise, Eban. I won't follow you," I said with all the gumption I had.

"Wish us luck," he added and gave the mustang a light flick on the rump and off he went down the hill.

But Major Lawson glanced from me to Boyd. "I'll look forward to more pan bread and rabbit around noon, if you boys are agreeable," he said and rode off after Eban.

Boyd put down his plate and stood. "I reckon if the Major wants some rabbit I'd best go hunting. Morning's always the best time to find rabbits. They'll be looking for breakfast like we are." And he walked off toward the ridge.

I put the cooking stuff away quick. I needed to hurry. Romy Manuel would likely leave his camp soon too. I couldn't count on him sticking around like he had yesterday. Besides I didn't know how long it would take for the men in Coloma to get organized and start out.

I walked to Rojo and started in on getting him saddled. When I'd cinched everything tight I pulled the shotgun from the scabbard and checked to make sure the caps hadn't fallen out and that it held a full load of buckshot in each barrel. Next I took Maggie's little gun from the pocket of my roll-up pants, checked it and slid it into the waistband near the small of my back. Ready as I'd ever be, I reached for the reins and realized my left hand trembled like the dickens again. I shook it hard hoping it would settle down. I must be sick or something, I thought.

"Are you the one the Lord chose to smite down that red shirted devil?"

I near jumped out of my skin. It dawned on me pretty quick Bug Riddle had snuck up behind me, but how the old man managed to get so close hobbling along on a crutch like he did I couldn't figure. Still I turned to face him. "Sir?" I asked, understanding his meaning well enough but set on not telling a soul, even a crazy old man, what I had planned.

"You're saddling up, checking your guns. I seen men hunt men before. You're hunting for that black-hearted son of Satan. I know. I've known since you got here." Bug spoke softly but then his eyes got wild. "You kill him boy. Send him straight to hell. You do it and the Lord will bless you, but if you ain't got the guts, or if he sneaks up on you like you aim to sneak up on him, you run to Bug Riddle. I'll be waiting, watching for that red shirted devil to ride into the river. You run, boy, before he pounds the life blood from the very pores on your face then stomps your bones underfoot like a normal man does kindling wood. You run. You run to me. You hear me, boy? You run to me!"

I could barely believe what I'd heard. Bug Riddle ranted like a madman but he'd figured out exactly what I planned. "I got the guts," I yelled. "I ain't going to run like no coward. I know where he is. I'll find him. I'll kill him." Bug stared at me, his face dark with rage. But he'd hit my sore spot hard. "I will," I added, louder than before and crammed my left hand into my pocket to calm the confounded shaking down some.

The hate in Bug's face eased into a nasty frown and his voice softened. "You kill him, boy. Blow his black heart to pieces with that scattergun then feed his wretched carcass to the buzzards, but bring the bloody shreds of that red shirt back here to old Bug Riddle so I can rest in peace. Will you do that for an old man, boy? Swear you'll bring me proof the devil is dead. Swear it, boy."

"I swear, sir. I'll bring you his shirt. Don't worry." I promised and felt some better right off. Now it sounded like Bug Riddle wanted to make sure I'd really taken care of what needed to be done to the man who broke his leg.

His tired eyes drilled into mine then, without another word, he turned and shuffled back to the hole he'd chopped in the earth, teetering on his crutch and waving the heavy Hawken rifle high over his head.

I started down the hill toward the river but stopped to look back at Bug. He sat quiet and still, not hacking with the hand ax, the big-bore rifle cradled in his left arm, his right hand on the trigger. The broken leg stretched out flat on the ground while the good one rested in the bottom of the hole he'd dug so that the knee bent at just the right height for a man who wanted to shoot someone down at the ford to rest his left elbow on so that he could steady his aim. Bug Riddle had dug himself a perfect place to sit and wait for Romy Manuel, and make the best shot he possibly could whenever the man who had tried to drown him in Weber Creek rode into the river.

It dawned on me that Bug might not be as off his rocker as he seemed. And in a flash I understood what must've happened that day along Weber Creek. Romy Manuel likely slipped up and beat Bug half to death before he braced Bug's foot on top of a log or rock then stomped down as hard as he could on the poor man's leg, snapping the bones in two like kindling. I shuddered when I thought about it. It must've hurt something awful. Then, adding insult to injury and figuring Bug would drown right quick, Romy Manuel drug him to the creek and tossed him in. I could even see him laughing as he watched poor Bug flop around in the stream, trying to keep his head above water.

Boyd said they called him Bug because when he got an idea in his head he couldn't get shed of it. Bug wanted revenge on Romy Manuel for what he did but Bug couldn't chase the varmint around on a busted leg so he decided to sit and wait. With all the gold mined here in these ravines, Romy Manuel was sure to show up sooner or later to strong arm one man or another into joining the mining cooperative or else to get off a good paying claim. When that day came Bug planned to blow his evil head right off.

I rode into the river and a hair-raising shiver bristled up my backbone. I spun in the saddle and looked back up the hill. At first I couldn't see Bug anywhere but I knew he sat right where I'd left him, watching and waiting. But he must have noticed me looking back because I saw him when he pumped the Hawken high in the air. I felt sorry for taking away the revenge that meant so much to him, but I'd set my mind on killing Romy Manuel no matter what. It had to be done. On the other hand I'd promised Bug and I'd keep my word. I'd bring the old man Romy Manuel's bloody red shirt at least. As I rode out of the water on the far bank I thought how it would all be over soon, but I sure wished I could stop my left hand from shaking.

##

At the road to Hangtown Creek I stopped. Straight ahead lay Coloma, and from somewhere in town Eban, Major Lawson and a posse of townsmen would soon come this way. I had to hurry so I rode on towards Hangtown Creek, past the redwoods to the west and the pines on the east. Soon the oaks rose on both sides of the trail. I edged Rojo into the woods and past a line of brush and scrub oak a hundred paces from the road.

I left the chestnut in the shade of an oak tree where plenty of grass grew. "You be real quiet while I'm gone, okay. I don't want that skunk to know anyone is here," I told him and Rojo bobbed his head and pawed at the ground like he understood. I knew that would be the best answer I would get. I pulled the shotgun from the scabbard and checked the firing caps under each hammer one more time. They both looked fine.

I gulped down a couple of deep breaths, squared my shoulders, and slipped off as quiet as a church mouse toward where I figured Romy Manuel's camp must be, the scattergun across my chest, right hand on the grip below the trigger guard, left hand on the stock under the barrels, both hammers cocked and ready to fire. My head swiveled from side to side. I ducked from tree to tree, glancing back a lot to make sure nobody tailed me. Little by little I made my way through the oaks close to the road so I could spot where his pinto had hit the trail yesterday.

Sneaking along as slow as I did it seemed like I'd never find this brigand's camp. Maybe I'd started too far down the road. A deep quiet hung all around me. No birds chirped from the trees. No squirrels chattered over an acorn. Not even a breeze blew in to rustle the oak leaves. The day had heated up, even in the shade, and sweat soaked my green shirt. My heart thumped so much I thought my chest would bust.

A loud crack rang out. I froze. My left hand trembled. But once more the deep hush closed back around me. I'd stepped on a branch and snapped it in two. If Romy Manuel heard it I'd face trouble, big trouble. I listened hard. I even held my breath, but heard nothing, no chirp, no chatter, not even a soft rustle in the trees. My right hand started to shake along with my left, jiggling the shotgun across my chest.

I pulled down one long breath, then another. I kept at it,

drawing air deep inside and letting it out slow, again and again. While I breathed I repeated to myself, *I'm a man now. I can do this.* Over and over I said it, until the words and my breathing merged into one throbbing pulse. Breathe in. *I'm a man now.* Breathe out. *I can do this.*

Time slowed to a crawl and so did the chant in my mind. My senses grew sharp. I could see everything now and all at once, not just in front of me but also to the sides and even behind. I could hear each sound for miles around, the splash of the river as it ran to the west, the flap of a hawk's wing high above. And I could feel the fire of life burning inside each living thing in the woods around me, like I belonged with them now, a part of the forest and no longer an outsider.

A mockingbird sang his high low call then trilled a short, sweet song. A squirrel chattered from a branch, quickly answered by another who skittered through the leaves, shaking the limbs above. A hoarse cry screamed down from a hawk soaring high above. The forest, so quiet before, now teemed with life. I realized my hands were still, the shaking gone. My fear had melted away like boiling water in a pot untended too long.

Romy Manuel hadn't heard the twig snap. Like all the animals in the forest I just knew. I walked on, confident, even cocky, a man with a tough job to do. Ahead I found a scuff mark on the forest floor. It came from the iron shoe of a horse, likely Romy Manuel's pinto. I walked toward the road and found several more clear prints plus a lot of oval dents in the ground where the horse had dug his hooves in as Romy spurred him onto the trail. I turned to follow the tracks back into the woods, to the camp of the man I came to kill.

A little deeper in the trees I caught sight of the pinto, hobbled in a small clearing. My heart thumped loud again. I breathed slow and easy and carefully crept across the open space to the horse. I held out my hand and let him smell me. At any time Romy Manuel could show up, looking for his mount, ready to ride off for whatever dirty work he had planned. I knew I had to stay alert and aware like I never had before.

I left the pinto and tiptoed to the scrub brush ahead, eased around a bush and peered into a campsite on the other side. Under a large oak I saw the ashes of a small campfire. Even from here they looked cold, like there hadn't been a fire there at least since yesterday. An old dented blue coffee pot lay on its side nearby. All in all something didn't seem right. If a man had camped here shouldn't I see more signs of him than a cold fire and an empty coffee pot?

Coaxing up as much courage as I could, I stuck my head farther out into the open and looked around real fast, swinging the scattergun along with my eyes. I stepped out of the brush and into the open. It took all the heart I could muster. If Romy Manuel saw me I'd be dead way before my time.

But no shot came, no Romy Manuel, nothing. I walked to the fire pit and felt the ashes like the Major had done. They were stone cold. Nobody had built a fire last night and banked the embers when they turned in so there would still be enough heat to restart it easily this morning. Nobody had slept here. Romy kept his horse here, that's all. But where had the slimy rattlesnake slithered off to, why, and with who?

I didn't know what to do. When I planned on sneaking up on this varmint at his campsite and shooting him, I hadn't thought that the guy wouldn't be here. A wave of relief rolled over me. Now I wouldn't have to kill a man after all, but as soon as that idea crossed my mind I turned sick right down to my toes. If I couldn't find Romy Manuel to shoot him then neither could Eban and Major Lawson and the scoundrel still might hurt Lacey. I'd let her down. I felt like a fool.

I felt worse when it dawned on me that if I stayed here Romy could slip up on me just like Bug Riddle had said. I needed to get away from the campsite quick, so I hustled back toward the trail thinking that if he did come back I could see him way before he got close. But when I got to the road I noticed something I'd missed before. Since I'd been so caught up in the deep gouges made when the horse rode off south after Romy Manuel spurred him on yesterday, I hadn't paid any attention to the other signs pressed into the dust—buggy tracks.

The light, narrow wheel marks stood out easily from the heavy, wide ruts a freight wagon like the one I drove by here most every day left on the trail. The prints of ironclad wheels hadn't seemed important before, after all Romy Manuel rode a horse. But now I could see it clear, somebody had stopped a buggy here and more than once, a lot more. Even the outline of horseshoes stood out where the horse waited in front of the buggy.

Boot prints started in the dust at the edge of the trail and stopped all at once right before the buggy tracks. Other boot prints appeared sideways to the road at about the same spot and vanished into the woods like they would if somebody climbed down from a buggy. The boots that made these prints had high heels and pointed toes. Unless I missed my guess they looked like the bottom side of special made, hand tooled Mexican riding boots—Romy Manuel's boots.

While I stared at the story unfolding in the dust it came to me that the only buggy I'd ever seen anywhere around these parts rode right by here yesterday looking for all the world like it was out of control, a real pretty lady named Dancy something or other crying out for help like a lost lamb cries for its mama. Up the road, past the curve where I'd seen Romy Manuel disappear yesterday, sat a clearing big enough for a buggy, or a freight wagon, to turn around in easy.

Another notion slapped me hard up the side of my head and I started to shiver. Romy Manuel and this Dancy lady had to be in cahoots. He probably spent every night in her room snuggling up with her in a big old feather bed. She'd pick him up here at night and drop him off in the morning. Eban said she sang at the Golden Nugget. If somebody who knew about the plans to nab this scoundrel blabbed about it there the chances she'd hear it were awful good. As sure as winter follows fall she'd tell everything she heard to her lover boy.

And here I stood, out in the open like a perfect fool, Dancy Bellotti and her murdering boyfriend likely slipping out of town and making their way here right now. Romy Manuel, armed to the teeth and as cold-blooded as a rattlesnake, would readily shoot anybody standing between him and where he kept the pinto—exactly where I stood. No wonder my whole body shook like a dried up cornstalk in a thunderstorm.

I hurried back into the woods like a hungry man late for supper and ducked behind the first big oak I found. Sweat poured into my eyes, stinging them. I yanked off the sombrero and wiped my face with my sleeve. A little while ago, when I'd first figured out Romy Manuel hadn't camped here, I'd been totally unsure what I should do, but now things seemed as clear as a glass of fresh spring water. The man Bug Riddle called a red shirted spawn of Satan would show up soon, planning on getting on his pinto and beating a fast path to someplace. I'd simply sit and wait for him.

I drew in in a deep breath and in my mind I heard the words from before, *I'm a man now.* Slowly I let the air out and like magic the words *I can do this* formed just like they had earlier. Again and again I breathed in the clean, fresh forest air. Again and again I let it slowly ease from my lips. Again and again the same words ran through my mind, *I'm a man now. I can do this. I'm a man now. I can do this.*

At first it sounded like a whisper on the wind, faint and far away, the steady clatter of a horse at a trot, growing louder, coming this way from Coloma. Soon came a rattle, a squeak, and the thump of an iron-rimmed wheel bouncing over a rut in the road. Dancy Bellotti's buggy, with Romy Manuel in it, headed this way. The time had come to prove I really am a man, that I really could do this.

I slipped around the tree so I could look down the road. I couldn't see the buggy yet but the sound of hoof beats grew steadily closer. My left hand started to shake again. I tightened my grip on the shotgun. I caught a glimpse of the stallion from yesterday, his hooves drumming on louder than even the thump of my thundering heart. In no time the buggy flashed by an opening in the forest cover.

The words came again. *I'm a man now. I can do this.* My breathing slowed in time with the words. The buggy stopped. I watched as fancy Mexican riding boots hit the trail. Flashes of red came through the leaves. The voice of a man speaking Mexican mixed with the soft sound of a woman laughing. Romy and Dancy were happy. They hadn't heard about Eban, Major Lawson and the posse.

I edged around the tree and leveled the shotgun at the red between the leaves, my fingers on the triggers to both barrels. As soon as the buggy left I'd shoot. I was a man now. I could do this. Then the red dropped to the ground, clear out of sight. A shot rang out. A ball ripped into me. I jerked back. The shotgun went off with a terrible boom, shattering limbs and leaves overhead. I screamed and tumbled to the ground, a fierce pain in my right arm.

A whip cracked and the buggy rumbled off. I stumbled to my feet, blood all over me—my blood. I had to get to Rojo. Romy Manuel would shoot me again if I didn't get away fast, but the gunshot stunned me. I didn't know where to find the chestnut. Still I ran. It was all I could do.

I'd lost the shotgun. It didn't matter. It was empty. The

sombrero had fallen off too and now sweat poured into my eyes again. I tried to wipe it out with the sleeve of my left arm, but ran headlong into something.

Oh God! Romy Manuel!

A hand grabbed the bandana around my neck. A fist slammed into my face, rattling my whole head. I squirmed, trying to get free but the fist smashed into my stomach, blowing air out of my lungs with a loud oomph. I wheezed, and gasped hard trying to suck more air back in. I needed to breathe. I needed to live. A hand slapped my face then the back of the hand fell harder still on my other cheek.

"Look at me, gringo. Look into my eyes." It was Romy Manuel, his voice slimy, oozing like rotten, moldy preserves from an old, crusty jar. My eyes stung from the sweat that poured into them. I couldn't look, but did manage a short gulp of air.

Another slap, followed by a backhand harder than before, "I said look into my eyes!" Now Romy Manuel screamed loud, wild. The moldy, rotten sound gone, replaced instead with the unholy roar of Satan. I opened my eyes, in spite of the sting of the sweat, terrified, trembling from nose to toe. Like Bug Riddle had said, Romy Manuel would pound the very lifeblood from the pores on my face. Then he'd likely break every bone in my body.

"Why you come after me, gringo, a little niño with a big shotgun? I kill you slow. I make you hurt till you beg to die." He laughed a dark, evil laugh. "Then I hurt you more."

I realized he'd left my hands free. The spawn of Satan held me up by the bandana around my neck. I'd tucked Maggie's little gun into the waistband of my roll-up pants at the small of my back when I left Bug's camp. I could get it—maybe. But my right arm was useless, shot up, throbbing, bleeding. I eased the left one behind my back.

Another swat spun my head around. "I question you. You answer. Now!"

I shook my head instead, knowing I might pass out soon. But I had to get to the gun before Romy did knock me senseless. I reached deep for whatever strength I could find, whatever courage my beat up soul had left, and spit into the face of the devil.

Romy Manuel howled and cursed loud in Mexican. Hate smoldered from dark, wicked eyes. Then he slowly wiped his face with the sleeve of his red shirt, and I pushed my left hand further behind my back until I found the handle of Maggie's gun. Another punch landed in my gut, harder than before. What little wind I still had blew out again. I wanted to double over, to gasp for air, but Romy Manuel held me up and punched me in the face again and again and again.

My mind faded with each blow. I couldn't take much more. I only wanted to die, when through the mist it came to me, *I'm a man now.* I sucked in air, hot, sweet air. *I can do this.* I blew it out through bloody, battered lips. *I'm a man now. I can do this.*

One of my eyes crept open. A will to live poured back into my heart. A resolve, steeled with grit I didn't know I had, overwhelmed my shattered body. Powered only by this deep-rooted desire to survive, without the help of a single thought, I kicked up hard with my right leg, square between Romy Manuel's legs. The wail of a thousand demons burst from Satan's mouth, I pulled Maggie's little gun, cocked it, poked it deep into Romy's gut and fired.

The little pistol popped. The sharp tang of burnt black powder filled the very air my lungs still needed so badly. Romy Manuel grunted, grabbed his gut with both hands and took a step back. His eyes grew wild and glazed with pain, but still the hate burned through, boiling up from his stinking, rotten soul.

The clatter of a horse and buggy came from the road and quickly stopped. A woman cried out in Mexican. It had to be Dancy Bellotti, calling for her red shirted lover. He barked back, a short two-word answer, Satan calling his Jezebel. Romy Manuel wasn't done, not by a long shot. He still had fight left in him. He wouldn't quit, not until I was dead—or he was. Now the woman would come to help.

I knew I had nothing left to fight with. Both guns empty, my body beaten, bruised, shot up and in no shape to even wrestle a woman, I had to run, find Rojo and ride as fast as I could away from here. I knew where the road was again, Dancy Belloti's buggy had stopped there, so I stumbled off toward where I thought I'd left my horse.

The forest, so open and free before, closed in around me, the deep silence smothering the very air I needed. I tripped and tumbled to the ground. Pain surged from the wound in my arm, my head throbbed, my jaw ached. I managed to stifle a scream. No matter what, even if Romy Manuel did find me, I refused to give that vermin the satisfaction of knowing how bad I hurt.

Loud voices talking in Mexican came from behind me somewhere. I couldn't understand the words exactly but somehow I knew Dancy Bellotti would bind up Romy Manuel's wound and help him to his horse. I pushed myself up and staggered on, but soon realized I'd lost my way. I had no idea where Rojo waited. If I couldn't find the chestnut before Romy Manuel came after me again I would soon be dead. My whole body trembled at the thought.

I ran on unsure where to go; lost, confused, wiping sweat from my eyes with a sopping left sleeve. Stumbling, falling, and getting up again, but nowhere could I find the horse. Then I heard a whip crack and the buggy rattle off. Dancy Bellotti had gone, heading back to Coloma. Romy Manuel would come soon. I had no time left to find Rojo. And there I saw the blood pooled on the forest floor—my blood.

I'd run in a circle and come back to the first place I'd fallen, but now I could still hear the rattle of the buggy along the trail. I could follow the sound toward Coloma, toward Rojo, toward my one last chance to live. I ran as fast as I could, sucking in air—*I'm a man now*—blowing it out—*I can do this.*

The clatter of the buggy faded fast and still I saw no sign of the chestnut. The killer tracked me now. I knew it. I had to find my horse. Rojo must be close, but where? Maybe if I called out Rojo would answer, but maybe he wouldn't and either way Romy Manuel would hear and know where to find me. With nothing else to do I ran on.

I heard the rustle of a horse following me, crackling the leaves underfoot as he came this way, the pinto, getting closer. I looked back and groaned. I'd left a clear trail to follow from the blood that dripped from my arm, one drop with every step I took, the dark red clear against the light brown forest floor. Like an idiot I'd led Romy Manuel straight to me. I whipped off my bandana and tied it around my wound, kicking myself for not doing it sooner and for making it so easy for that festering maggot to find me.

I had only one chance now—I had to find the chestnut. "Rojo, where are you?" I cried. No answer came, but the hoof beats from Romy's pinto grew louder. "Rojo, talk to me, please!" I imagined a wicked grin covering the face of the devil right now, and I hated to give that vicious butcher any more pleasure for his evil deeds but I had no choice. I was desperate. But Rojo didn't answer.

Panic crept into my very bones. My left hand shook wildly when I wiped the sweat from my forehead once more.

Through half closed eyes I saw it, a scuff in the forest floor, and another past it, and still another after that, the track of a horse— the track of Rojo. I wheeled right to follow the trail and finally saw him still tied to the oak tree. I'd never been so happy to see a horse in my life. "I hope you're ready to run," I whispered. My life depended on Rojo now—him and God.

I freed the reins, crawled into the saddle, turned the chestnut toward the road to Coloma and nudged him to a slow walk, sneaking across the open ground under the oaks beside clumps of scrub brush along the way I'd come. I hoped with all my heart that Romy Manuel wouldn't hear Rojo as he stepped through the leaves, at least not until I'd made it to the trail.

Ahead I could see a small stain of blood on the ground where I'd stopped and tied the bandana around my arm. I drew in more clean air. *I'm a man now.* I let it out slow. *I can do this.* But my left hand, the one that held the reins, began to shake again, trembling like never before. *I'm a man now. I can do this.* The words rolled through my brain again and again yet the shiver continued. The words that once calmed my fear no longer helped. I looked around and saw nothing, no one. Everything seemed peaceful, natural— everything except the stillness. The creatures here had hidden, quiet, scared, just like before I'd become one of them, before I belonged in the woods. Someone else had come, someone who didn't belong.

Romy Manuel!

"Hiyah," I yelled and kicked Rojo's flanks as hard as I could. A loud boom split the quiet. Buckshot whizzed behind my head, shredding the leaves of nearby trees without mercy. My horse raced toward the road. Loud hoof beats came from my left, the pinto with the devil on his back raced to cut me off.

"Run, Rojo, run," I yelled, but the chestnut already had hit full stride. I kept the reins loose, giving him his head. He knew the way and galloped with a burning eagerness to run free. I quickly stole a glance at Romy Manuel heading for the same spot along the road that I did, the place I'd left the trail when I came into the woods. I had the shorter distance to run. I would make the trail first, but Romy Manuel would be right on my tail.

I tucked my head as low as possible over Rojo's neck, trying to give the smallest target I could. The shotgun blast had been close, too close, and Romy still carried the scattergun in his hand with one barrel left to fire. I'd been lucky once, but knew that the odds of him missing a second shot were slim.

Rojo broke from the trees and onto the road with a new burst of power, galloping full out toward the American River. I dared another glance to the trail behind me. Romy Manuel came fast, the shotgun still in his hand, a shredded white petticoat tied around his gut. The pinto's head bobbed up and down just like Rojo's did, his nose flared wide as he drew in air and his hooves threw clods of dirt high each time they dug into the hard clay trail.

But I had a lead of about ten horse lengths. Maybe Rojo could run as fast as the pinto, and hopefully a little faster. Still, Romy Manuel could shoot me with the scattergun anytime, but from a horse moving that fast he might miss. At least that's what I told myself, but if the buckshot did hit me the blast would tear my back apart, blow me clean out of the saddle and likely kill me outright.

I shuddered. "Go Rojo. Hurry," I yelled and gave him a kick, desperately hoping that he could run even faster.

Up ahead the trail turned to the left. I'd made a lot of trips along this stretch of road, sometimes hauling supplies into Coloma but almost always with a heavy wagonload of lumber on the way back. I knew every turn, bump, and rut from Hangtown Creek to the American River and just past this next curve the trail got steeper and the turns sharper and closer together.

Rojo wheeled to the west, still running at a full gallop, leaning into the trail sure-footed and strong. After Maggie had left him cooped up in the stable so much lately he welcomed the chance to run free and fast again like any good horse would. But I thought it awful strange that while having Romy Manuel on my tail scared me out of my gourd, Rojo ran on like he'd never had so much fun, and if I lived I'd be eternally grateful to him for that.

Another curve loomed, this one to the right. We swung into it at full gallop when, directly in front of me, square in the middle of the road and going way slower than Rojo, I saw Dancy Bellotti's buggy. I knew I couldn't slow Rojo down at all. Instead I had to let him run, trusting him to find the best way past the slow moving shay. When I got closer she looked back at me with an ugly sneer, grabbed a buggy whip and cracked it over Rojo's head. The chestnut shied back and slowed to a trot.

I kicked his flanks. "Go Rojo, go fast," I yelled as loud as I could and kicked again. He sped up but once more the whip came out. This time I pulled the reins to the right and rode close to the edge of the trail where the road dropped off into the pines. Dancy turned the buggy to block my way and again Rojo slowed.

But I yanked the reins left. Rojo charged back along the other side of the buggy. Dancy still had the quirt in her hand and this time she swung at me. It cracked beside my right ear, snapping loud and leaving a ringing in my head. By now the stallion ran all out but Rojo still pulled up even with him. The whip cracked across my back. I screamed and dared a quick glance behind me. Romy Manuel rode right on Rojo's tail, still holding the shotgun and coming fast.

Dancy Bellotti raised the whip once more. Somehow my bloody, useless right arm shot up to block the blow. The leather thong at the end of the lash wrapped around my forearm and I managed to grab it and hold on. The dark haired Jezebel pulled with all the strength she had, determined to slow me up. Yet in spite of the searing pain in my arm I held on with every bit of grit I had. Rojo pulled ahead of the stallion now and Dancy Bellotti had to latch onto one of the iron struts that held up the buggy top to keep from being yanked out.

Rojo kept running strong and he tugged her up from her seat. With one hand on the strut and one on the whip she teetered at the side of the buggy, ready to fall out. Stubborn and stupid, she refused to let go of either one, so I wrapped the reins around my saddle horn, grabbed the whip with my left hand and jerked it as hard as I could. Dancy screamed like a cornered bobcat, and tumbled head over heels from the buggy slamming face first onto the hard clay of the road right in front of Romy Manuel and slowing the pinto down. I unwound the whip from my shot-up right arm and dropped it. Meanwhile the buggy bounced wildly behind the stallion, and Rojo easily pulled ahead of him. The trail in front of me was clear.

I heard her yelling and had to look, but the buggy blocked her from view. When the pinto raced past the stallion he'd lost ground back to about the same ten lengths he'd been behind earlier. I let out a long sigh. The scrape with Dancy Bellotti had been close, way too close. Still I didn't feel one bit bad for having dumped a woman onto the road like I did. An ungentlemanly thing to do for sure, but she would've got me killed if Romy caught up, and he almost did. Heck, she's lucky the fall didn't break her rotten neck.

The river was close and the road swerved sharply back and

forth here. I let Rojo run free, trusting him to keep his footing when the trail came close to the low lying pines on the right. One slip and both of us could tumble off the road. I knew that a fall might kill me outright, but if I reined in Rojo and took the turns at an easier pace Romy Manuel could catch me. That would mean an even more painful death.

I stole another glance over my shoulder. The pinto stayed put at ten lengths behind, and Romy Manuel still had the scattergun in his hand. Not far ahead the road would make a hard turn left into town, but to the right a smaller horse path led to the ford across the American River. There Bug Riddle waited on top of the ridge with his Hawken rifle. I pulled Rojo hard onto the horse path, wondering if the old man would even recognize me. Would he know Romy Manuel trailed me? And even if he did, it was a long, hard shot all the way from the top of the ravine to the river. Could he make that shot? I had to hope so. If he didn't my goose was cooked.

Rojo found the path without losing a step, hooves thundering, pounding out a spellbinding beat that throbbed in my head. His front feet hit the ground one right after the other, then the back ones did the same thing. The steady rhythm pulsed through my body over and over again, and, together with the easy sway of Rojo's back, I felt a part of him. Rojo and I were one.

I relaxed into the smooth, easy movements a rider must make on a fast horse. Even my breathing worked in harmony with Rojo's gait. Breathe in. *I'm a man now.* Breathe out. *I can do this.* My fear melted away, like it had in the forest. I felt safe—until I looked back.

"Go Rojo!" I yelled. I'd relaxed way too much. Romy Manuel had caught up.

I could see the ford now. It was close. I knew that as soon I rode into the water Rojo would slow down. He had to. No horse can cross a river this deep at anything other than a walk. All Romy Manuel had to do was shoot me in the back. Fear crowded my mind again. Bug Riddle was my only chance now. But what if the old man had fallen asleep, or couldn't decide if it really was Romy Manuel behind me, or maybe he'd just out and out miss the shot. Bug won that rifle a long time ago. Maybe his eyes were gone. Maybe he'd lost his touch.

"Oh Lord, please!" I cried, thinking how much I wanted to see Lacey again.

But my path was set. I had no choice. I pulled Rojo to the left and splashed into the river. He slowed to a walk almost at once but plowed on step by step toward the north bank. I waved wildly hoping Bug would see me. It was all I could do to save myself, but would Bug even recognize me without the sombrero? My life was in his hands now—or God's.

I scanned the ridge, looking for him, silently praying for all the help I could get.

"Gringo!" A shiver ran down my back. Romy Manuel called, his voice full of hate.

I spun in the saddle. He sat on the pinto at the water's edge, blood oozing through the petticoat, the shotgun pointed at the sky, his finger on the trigger, ready to shoot.

There was nothing I could do. I was helpless, a sitting duck in the river and Romy knew it. My thoughts went back to Lacey. "I love you." I whispered. I turned Rojo around in the middle of the stream. I didn't want to be shot in the back. I wanted to face my fate head on.

"You, a niño, a filthy gringo, have killed me," he snarled. "But you will get to hell before I do." Gut shot and bleeding bad he was right. He'd die soon, but I'd die first.

The scattergun hammer clicked loud. I closed my eyes. I didn't want to know when it would happen.

The shotgun boomed.

"Oh God, I'm dead." I screamed.

Another shot echoed across the river.

Buckshot splattered like hail in the water all around me. Holy Moses, I thought. My eyes popped opened in time to see Romy Manuel topple from the pinto and plop flat on his back like a hundred pound sack of oats that tumbled off a wagon.

I looked back up the hill and it sure seemed like I heard Bug Riddle shout, "The devil's dead." He stood up and pumped the Hawken high over his head. I waved. Bug had done it. He'd saved my bacon and I was awful grateful to him. It dawned on me exactly how close I'd really come to buying the farm. The tremble in my left hand suddenly swept up my arm and shook my whole body, and as fast as it had come over me the shaking stopped.

I looked back toward the south shore and stroked the chestnut's neck. "I'm sorry, Rojo, but we got to go back," I said. Obligingly he plowed through the current to the bank. I slid out of the saddle and went over to the body of Romy Manuel. He didn't look so fearsome with a hole in the middle of his forehead and his blood, brains and hair splattered all over the ground.

I pulled my buck knife out of my pocket and knelt down. Bug Riddle had saved my life and earlier today I'd made him a promise. Now there was nothing on God's green earth that could keep me from bringing the devil's red shirt to him. I slashed off the petticoat, hacked off the buttons on the front, then rolled Romy over and ripped the shirt from his back.

It came to me that Bug must have hit him while the shotgun pointed straight up in the air, right after he'd cocked it. That's why the shot fell all around me like it had, but I sure couldn't figure why I heard the shogun fire before Bug's rifle did, almost like the rifle ball went faster than the sound of the gun.

I stuffed Romy's shirt into a saddlebag, and started to climb on Rojo when a man riding another pinto splashed into the river from the north side. He looked like the same man Bug had almost shot the first day I got to his camp, the guy with the guitar. He rode past me with only a tug at the brim of his black hat and stopped beside Romy Manuel, hopped to the ground, kicked the body over with his boot and growled a couple of words in Mexican that I couldn't understand. He made the sign of the cross and spit into the face of Romy Manuel.

With a shake of his head he turned back to me. "He was my countryman, but still he was a bad man, a stinking coyote," he said with a sneer. "No one will weep for him."

He went to Romy's pinto and took the reins. "A fine horse, si?" he asked, and without waiting for my answer he tied him to Rojo's saddle. "He is yours, senor," he went on. "You are the winner. You have lived. El Diablo is dead." He noticed Romy's shotgun lying on the ground. He picked it up and stuffed it into Rojo's scabbard without a word then walked back to his own horse, pulled the guitar from his back and leaped into the saddle.

"Adios, Senor," he cried and turned the pinto toward Coloma. "Vaya con Dios," he yelled over his shoulder and rode away. Soon I could hear him singing the same song I'd heard last night right before I fell asleep, the sad one about the man and his girl, Carmelita.

"Vaya con Dios," I mumbled, mostly to myself, remembering how God really must have been with me today. I looked up to the sky. "Thank you, sir," I said softly. There wasn't any use to explain it all. God should know what the thanks were for. Still, I was thinking hard about how lucky I'd been to get away from Romy Manuel in the first place, and then how I'd run like a scared dog, and if it hadn't been for Bug Riddle I'd be stone dead right now. When it came right down to it I was nothing more than a yellow coward and didn't deserve to live. God, I felt rotten.

Two vultures circled slowly over the river valley. I ignored them. They were welcome to whatever was left of Romy Manuel.

9

I'd spent all morning with the Sheriff and a whole bunch of other men. They wanted to know everything that happened, where it happened, why it happened. It all never seemed to end. But back where I first saw Romy Manuel get out of Dancy Bellotti's buggy I'd found my sombrero and the shotgun I'd dropped.

Now I'd pulled the wide-brimmed Mexican hat low again so people would have a hard time seeing the pounding I took yesterday. One eye had already swollen shut and the other came darn close. Ugly scabs had formed on my lips and my whole face had puffed up like a loaf of fresh baked bread and was covered in big purple welts. I felt awful and knew I looked it.

Web Lawson acted real proud of how I'd managed to stand up to a beating from a thug like Romy Manuel and still have enough sense left to get away and lead him straight into Bug Riddle's gun sight. He was wrong. I hadn't been man enough to do the job I set out to do and only my good luck, or a whole lot of help from above, allowed me to live at all.

And at first Eban had been as mad as I'd ever seen him, but he'd cooled down some now. Still, Eban was right. Deep down I knew it. After all, nothing worked like I'd planned—not by a long shot. Romy Manuel could have killed me outright back along the road. I got a chance to get away only because Romy wanted to toy with me and make me suffer more. And I ran like a scared rabbit with a big dog on his tail.

When we got near Hangtown I'd slowed Rojo down some to let Eban and Major Lawson ride ahead, figuring that since most of the men here knew Eban real good they'd be more likely to notice the beat up fellow in the Mexican sombrero riding Maggie's horse if I rode with them. There ain't no denying I fretted something awful about how folks would react to my looks, and why I looked this way. Everybody around was bound to find out what a yellow coward I really am, but I stewed most over how Lacey would feel about me now.

I rode slow up Hangtown's Main Street, my head down, back slumped. A crowd of fresh-off-the-boat miners milled about outside the Round Tent Saloon, yelling, arguing, a lot of them already drunk. I could hear bits and snips of what they were saying. The name Reid Harrison came up a lot, usually with a curse and followed by a nasty comment about the mining cooperative. These men were mad, most just realizing how much money they had been bilked out of by Romy Manuel and his cohorts.

It was a sad thing. Mining was hard work, but what knocked me for a loop was that these men never even had the foggiest notion that the mining cooperative had been lying to them from day one. Those crooks had stuffed their own pockets with a fat share of the miner's hard earned gold while telling folks they put that money into new finding new claims and prospecting new territory in order to make the miners even more money.

Bags of gold had been crammed in every nook and cranny in Reid Harrison and Frank Barney's offices. Romy Manuel had his share stashed away with his Jezebel, Dancy Bellotti. It added up to one tidy sum—more than any reasonable miner could spend in a hundred years of high-toned living, even in a rich city like New York—or so folks said.

After I passed the crowd I relaxed some. But as much as I didn't want anybody in town to see me all beat up like this, I still had to face Lacey and pretty darn soon. Eban and the Major already rode across the log bridge. I'd gone out and found Lacey's pa like she wanted, and maybe that would make her happy, but she'd likely take one look at my ugly mug and realize what a lily-livered chicken I really am. She'd be right too. The thought scared me almost as much as facing Romy Manuel had.

When I rode up to the bridge I could see her in her yellow dress, racing down the steps from the cabin, her blonde pigtails flapping as she turned and ran downhill as fast as she could. "Papa! Papa," she yelled, loud and happy.

She wanted her Papa now, I thought. Doesn't she want to see me?

"Lacey, honey, I'm so glad you're safe," the Major whooped. He reached down and scooped her up onto the pinto I'd gotten from Romy Manuel.

And firmly wrapped in her Papa's arms, her face peering

over his shoulder, she noticed me for the first time. Her jaw dropped like a rock. My one good eye locked onto her. I knew she saw what I looked like. How could she not see the black, swollen eyes, the purple scabs, and the yellow steak down my back? The surprise on her face melted in a heartbeat, pushed away by a frown that showed her utter disgust. I ducked my head behind the brim of my hat, yanked Rojo around and tore back toward the cafe.

"Tom," she yelled. "Come back."

But I ignored her. Her face held all the scorn, shock and pure horror of seeing a chicken-hearted wimp whose face had been destroyed by a miserable varmint. She had her Papa back now. She had no use for me anymore. I understood. I wasn't stupid—just gutless. Still, it hurt. It hurt bad.

I tied the chestnut to the rail in front of the cafe and went to the door. It was latched from the inside, the closed sign hanging behind the glass. Eban rode up and stopped beside Rojo.

"Tom, are you all right?" he asked and I could hear the worry in his voice. I didn't know how to answer. I wasn't all right. Maybe I'd never be all right.

"I'm fine," I lied. Lying was easy now, easier than telling Eban the truth, easier than admitting what a chicken-hearted milksop I really am.

"Maggie and Lacey want to see you, son. Why don't you—?"

"Nobody wants to see me!" I screamed at the top of my lungs. Didn't Eban understand? Nobody would want to see me looking like this. And I sure didn't want either of them staring at my ruined face. The memory of Lacey as she gawked at me over her Papa's shoulder slapped me in the chin again. No! Lacey sure as heck didn't want to see me.

Eban shrugged. "Well, I'll make some excuse for you. Why don't you get some rest," he said real gentle and reached over and grabbed Rojo's reins. "I'll take your horse down to the stable for you."

Dang, I thought. I realized I'd been so wrapped up in my own shortcomings that I'd already forgotten all about poor Rojo and likely would have left him tied to the rail all night, unfed and uncared for. It was a terrible way to treat an animal, and after Rojo saved my life just yesterday it made what I almost did doubly bad. I felt more rotten now than I had before. "Thanks, Eban," I said and this time I told the truth.

He turned the mustang and started toward the stable with Rojo right behind him. "Good night, son," he called back.

I felt alone. I'd asked for it yet now the thought of being by myself bothered me. It wasn't that I was lonely but more that I needed someone to tell me I wasn't ugly, that what I'd done was worth the pounding I took and that I really wasn't a yellow-bellied mouse. I needed Lacey but she was with her Papa, and like a fool I'd just refused to go and see her. With my head hung low I shuffled to the back door of the cafe.

##

A bright light shone in my face, so bright I couldn't see.

"Tom! Tom can you hear me?" Lacey called me. I could hear her easy but she stood far away on top of a cliff, hidden somewhere in the glare. To get to her I had to climb the rocky face of the bluff. I had no choice. I pulled my way up hand over hand. When I looked down a river of flame blazed below me with smoke and steam billowing up into the gulch. One slip and I would tumble into the inferno and burn to a crisp in no time.

"Tom! Tom Marsh, you answer me!" Lacey yelled again, loud and angry.

I tried to call to her but couldn't say a word. My jaw hurt. My whole face hurt. I climbed faster. Almost at the top a hand grabbed my leg and yanked. Someone wanted to drag me off the cliff, to pull me into the fire. I looked down, straight at Romy Manuel, a bloody hole in the middle of his forehead. With an evil laugh the killer tugged me toward the fires of hell.

"Go away!" I yelled and kicked the varmint right in the nose. That sent Romy tumbling back to the burning chasm below, shrieking like a banshee while he fell.

"I'm not going anywhere until you open this door," Lacey shouted. She still sounded mad and started pounding on something, like she was hammering nails.

I realized I wasn't hanging off the side of the cliff anymore. I forced my right eye open. "Oh Lord," I wailed. I was in the cafe. It had all been a dream. Lacey waited outside the back door beating on it. I'd better let her in. "Hold on," I yelled. "I'm coming."

Bright sunlight burned through the windows. I'd slept way late. Usually I got up before dawn. I sat up on the edge of the cot.

Every part of my body hurt and I groaned when I grabbed my pants and slid them on. They were filthy and covered in blood. My shirt was worse, plus it had a hole in the sleeve where Romy Manuel shot me. I threw it in the corner so Lacey wouldn't see it. The last of my new shirts lay on the table. I struggled into it and pulled on my boots.

At the door I reached for the latch but paused. The memory of Lacey's face when she saw me yesterday filled my mind. The way her jaw dropped, her eyebrows jumped up on her forehead, the horror and disgust she must have felt all flooded back to me. Why had she come here then? She had her Papa back. She knew what I looked like, how I'd run away from Romy Manuel like a stinking yellow coward. Did she come out of pity? Politeness? Charity?

"I can hear you, Tom. I know you're at the door. I want to see you. Please let me in." She'd stopped yelling, her voice soft and sweet like before I left, before Romy Manuel.

I flipped up the latch and pulled open the door. My head dropped down to hide the beating I took and the shame I felt from what it had caused me to do, but Lacey walked right up anyway. I saw her yellow dress swaying as her hips moved. I couldn't help it. I had to raise my eyes. She looked so pretty with her blond hair tied back in a bun like the first time I saw her. Her blue eyes shone bright like a lamp on a moonless night.

"Oh, Tom," she sighed and put a soft hand to my cheek. "Look what that horrible man did to you, and all because you wanted to help me find my Papa."

"It's nothing," I mumbled, lying again. "Just a couple of bumps and bruises."

Her arms wrapped around me, her head buried in my chest. I reached behind her with my good arm and pulled her closer. I didn't understand her at all, but right now it didn't matter, nothing mattered but holding her tight.

When she pulled away her eyes looked down to the floor. She brushed past me. "Why there's no fire. You haven't had breakfast." She picked up the coffee pot. "Not even coffee. I'll fix you some."

I sat at the table and watched her start a fire under a burner then fill the coffee pot and set it on the stove. Her eyes didn't find me once the whole time.

I knew why. Still, I had to ask. "What's wrong, Lacey? Is it how I look, or because I'm a yellow coward?" There, I'd said it.

She whirled. "Oh God, no! You're not any of that!" she shot back with a fury. "It's worse. It's a lot worse." Her face wrinkled up like it did when she was going to cry, but she didn't. Instead she walked to the table, sat beside me and took my hand.

She'd confused me. Maybe something else had happened or maybe she just didn't want to hurt my feelings. Somehow neither choice made me feel any better. But I waited for her to tell me what she meant.

She looked straight into the one eye I had that worked. "You saved my Papa. He told me how you found him. He says he would have died if you hadn't come looking for him—"

"But Lacey, I didn't—"

"Yes, you did. You're too modest. You found my Papa and you did it for me." She sniffed and I could see a tear in the corner of her eye. "Eban said you'll heal up as good as new, and I know you will. Papa is so proud of the way you stood up to that awful man after the beating he gave you. He thinks you're a real hero and so do I. It isn't your face, honest. And you aren't a coward. You're the bravest man I know. I'm flattered you'd get into so much trouble for me, any girl would be, but . . ."

The rattle of a freight wagon came from the street outside the cafe and I heard Eban yelling out for the mules to stop. Someone knocked loud at the front door.

"It's Papa," Lacey said. "He wants to talk to you. I'll let him in."

She stood and hugged me tight before running into the dining room. I heard the bell over the door jingle and Web Lawson said something real soft to her. When the door closed the sound of heavy boots thumped on the floor and Lacey's pa soon walked into the kitchen, still limping, a box wrapped in brown paper under one arm.

"How do you feel today, son?" he asked.

"I guess I'm okay, sir," I said.

The Major pulled out a chair at the table and sat. The coffee began to sizzle. I went to the stove and yanked the pot off the burner.

"I'll get you some coffee, Major." I offered, then quickly found two cups, filled them, and pulled out a chair across the table from him.

The Major took a sip of the hot brew, all the while staring right into my battered face. "Wear those bruises with pride, son," he said with a smile. "They are the marks of courage so rare that only a few others share it. To go after a man like Romy Manuel took incredible heart. But when all looked lost you refused to accept defeat. You should be extremely proud."

"Thank you, sir," I mumbled, wondering if the Major jawed me for Lacey's sake. "But you didn't come here to talk about my bruises."

He chuckled. "No, I certainly didn't, but I do mean what I said. Your face will heal and if a mark or two remains it will only be a reflection of that courage."

"If you say so, sir," I muttered looking down, "but I ran away. I'm a coward. There ain't no way out of it."

Major Lawson stared at me hard, his face as serious as I'd ever seen it. "Yes," he agreed, "you ran away, but if you hadn't you would've died right there. Soldiers retreat when they're in an untenable situation. Escaping from certain death isn't an act of cowardice, son, it's good sense. But you really showed true bravery at the river. When you were trapped in the rushing water you turned your horse around to face your fate. Overcoming fear is the mark of a man with courage."

"I didn't want to be shot in the back, sir," I admitted.

The Major smiled. "I doubt if you know this. Eban told me last night. Without your sombrero Bug Riddle had no idea it was you when you rode into the river. And until you turned your horse and faced Romy Manuel, he also didn't know that the killer was behind you, ready to shoot. Bug's an old man. His eyes aren't that good anymore. Frankly, I don't know how he ever made that shot. The Good Lord must have guided the rifle ball, and I'd like to think He did it because of the courage you showed."

I gulped. I'd thought all along that I'd been lucky. Now I was sure. And what the Major said about courage settled on me like a warm blanket on a cold winter night. Still, I couldn't really believe all of what he said about me being brave, but somehow I felt better anyway.

"I guess you know I want to talk about Lacey, don't you?" he said, changing the subject.

"You do, sir?" I sputtered and a deep dread swept over me.

"My daughter is terribly fond of you, and that puts me in an awkward position. You see, I've been ordered back to Washington and I want Lacey with me, like any father with a fifteen-year-old girl would. We're due to leave the fifth of next month. Frankly, I was surprised that she put up such a fight about it when I told her last night. She's never done such a thing before."

My heart sank, and just when I'd started to think she still liked me. I knew what the Major was about to say. "Lacey's going back with you, isn't she?" I moaned.

"Yes, Tom. I think it's best. She's a wonderful girl and there are so many opportunities for her there that don't exist out here. She knows that as well as I do and she loves me very much, as I'm sure you know, but if you would ask her she would stay here with you, I think."

"You mean get married like Maggie and Joshua?"

"Yes, that's exactly what I mean."

"Holy Moses!" I exclaimed.

"I don't want you to misunderstand me, Tom. You've just saved my life and I will be eternally grateful to you, but in spite of that I don't think I could find a finer young man for my daughter. I know how much you care for her and how far you will go to make her happy. I'm sure she knows that too. But I think you are both too young for the responsibilities of a family."

"Maggie got married when she was about Lacey's age and she's done fine."

"Yes, but I understand she's had more than her share of hard times. Still, she's a wonderful woman and she loves you very much."

"Yes sir. Maggie's darn special. That's for sure."

"Like I said, I owe you a lot, son. Just like there are opportunities for Lacey back east that don't exist here, there are opportunities for a smart, ambitious young man like you. How would you like to go with us? You could stay in our home in Washington. I could get you into a fine school where you could gain some polish in the ways of polite society. I believe you would do quite well. Then, in a few years, when you've established yourself, you and Lacey could be married with a handsome ceremony in a beautiful church. How does that sound?"

"Gee," I mumbled and took a sip of coffee. Major Lawson had hit me harder than Romy Manuel ever could. I had so much to mull over and I had to do it real sudden like. "Back east would Lacey be able to ride around in a fancy buggy like Dancy Bellotti did?" I asked.

"Yes, Tom. I've been promised a promotion so there might

be an even nicer carriage."

"Would she wear pretty dresses and hats with feathers in them and stuff?"

"If she wants, certainly."

I gulped. I had to ask this question but the answer was sure to hurt. "Can she marry a rich guy and live in a big house with servants to cook and open the door and do the wash and things?"

"I don't know who she'll marry, but a pretty girl like her will be very popular in the best circles of Washington society. She'll likely have her choice of a number of well-placed young men." The Major's tone was calm and matter of fact. I knew he told the truth.

But that wasn't the worst of it. He was right about everything he said. Life for a woman here in the mining country was hard, real hard. Maggie talked about it all the time, but Maggie loved it and she had a toughness that was special. Lacey was a pretty tough girl but she didn't have Maggie's sand. Not many did.

And the one thing that ate at me most was the part about how pretty she was. There ain't no use to deny it. She had to be the best looking girl I'd ever seen, and I knew she'd be one of the prettiest back in Washington. The boys would all come to see her, like they came here to the cafe. It wasn't for the food, but just for a chance to look at Lacey and maybe talk to her.

Back east she could marry a rich fellow and live in a fine house in a fancy city. That would fit her a lot better than marrying me and living in a log cabin at the edge of the wilderness with nothing but rough miners around everywhere. No, Lacey needed a chance to make the best she could for herself, and that would come in Washington City, not Hangtown.

Sure, I loved her. I loved her a lot. And the Major said I could go with them and live in his house. But deep down I knew that I belonged here. I loved the wildness of the place, the quiet of the forest, the might of the Sierra, the grit of the miners. Back east I'd be like a fish out of water. I wouldn't know how to act around all those city folks anyhow. Sure, I'd like to see Washington City someday, even New York too, but not right now, maybe when I got older.

When I added it up the answer came clear. Lacey would leave today. I'd stay. It was rotten luck. I felt worse than I did when Pa died, but Pa had been drinking so much right before he went that it almost seemed a relief somehow. There was no upside to this. Chances were darn good that I'd never see her again. And the hardest part of it all was that it was best for both of us.

"I'd like to say goodbye to her, sir," I looked down and drained my coffee. I didn't want to face the Major right now.

"Of course, Tom," he replied and slid the box he had brought in with him across the table. "This is for you, son. It's not much thanks from a man whose life you saved but perhaps it may save yours one day. Go ahead. Open it."

I looked up at him. His expression was serious, like it usually was. "You don't owe me anything, sir. I only did what anybody would do," I said.

"Anyone might have saved my life, but only you did it. I'm sure that with your nature you'll run into more situations where you're in great danger. I want to know that I've done what I can to keep you as safe as possible. Open the box, son."

Major Lawson's words felt like an order. "Yes sir," I replied and tore the brown paper away to see a beautifully made maple box with a brass plate across the front that said *Patent Arms Manufacturing Co., Paterson, N.J.* "Sir, it's your Paterson Colt. I can't take this."

"Oh yes you can. I'm in the army, remember. They will be happy to issue a new pistol to a Lieutenant Colonel who has done so much for his country in the wilds of California. Besides, you need it more than I will in Washington. All your supplies are in the box, lead, a bullet mold, gun oil, caps, gunpowder, a cleaning rod, a second cylinder and some rags. It's yours, son, and may God bless you for all you've done for my daughter and me."

"Lacey, sir?" I asked. I didn't remember doing anything for Lacey, except find her Pa.

"Maybe you'd best ask Maggie to explain that one." The Major smiled and stood. "I also left you my saddle and all the gear with it. Your new pinto is a fine animal. You'll need the tack and I can't take it back east." He waved his arm toward the street. "Come, Eban is waiting. It's a long ride to Sacramento City then downriver to San Francisco. I'm sure he'd like to get started."

"Yes sir," I said. I left the pistol box on the table and followed Lacey's pa outside.

She sat beside Eban on the wagon seat, staring at the cafe door, waiting for me to come out. Her eyes, however, went first to her Papa. I knew she wanted to see if he still carried the box wrapped in brown paper. If he did, I'd be going to Washington with her, and if the box was gone I'd stay here. Her face fell, but she bravely looked straight at me and wrestled up a tiny smile.

I climbed up on the axle hub and pulled her to me with my left hand. My good eye closed when her arms went around my neck. In spite of the pounding my lips had taken I kissed her hard. It hurt like the dickens, but not nearly as much as the pain of losing her. She held on to me so tight I thought she wouldn't let go. That would be fine.

"Lacey, we have to go, Honey," the Major said finally.

She pulled back enough to look me in my good eye. "I'll write you. I promise," she whispered. I knew she choked back tears, determined not to cry this time of all times.

"I'll write you too," I said, knowing it didn't matter. I'd never see her again, but I'd miss her, maybe every day for the rest of my life. It sure seemed that way.

Eban wanted to start the mules. I felt a hand on my shoulder and looked. Major Lawson needed to board the wagon. I hopped to the ground. "Goodbye, sir," I said.

"Take care of yourself, Tom. I hope we meet again."

When Lacey's pa climbed into the seat Eban cracked the reins. 'Get up, mules," he yelled and the wagon rumbled down the road, taking Lacey away forever. She turned and waved. I waved back then stood and stared after her until the wagon finally rolled out of sight.

A soft hand settled on my shoulder. I spun. Maggie had been standing behind me, quietly waiting while Lacey disappeared down the road. She carried little Josie wrapped in a blanket in her right arm, and looked great like always. Her red hair glowed in the sunlight and the sparkle in her green eyes reminded me how much I'd missed her.

"Hi, Maggie," I stammered, trying my best not to sound glum.

She looked deep into my face. "Oh, my," she said and put her fingers on my neck under the one ear where I hadn't been beat on as much. "I'm really proud of you and what you did, but, Lord, I hope you never do anything like that again."

"Proud!" I blurted. "But Maggie—"

"Thank God you're still alive. I don't know what made you go after such a vicious killer alone like that. It took a lot of guts, but the smartest thing you did was to run away. If you hadn't, that man would have killed you and Josie would have to grow up without a godfather."

"But Lacey—"

"Lacey! Don't you know how much that girl loves you and how proud she is of you? She would've married you if you'd asked her. But you didn't, and my guess is you thought living in the gold country would be too hard for her right now. I'm proud of you for that too. To let a girl that special, someone that you care about as much as you do Lacey, go all the way back east because it would be better for her, now that's courage."

I shrugged. I didn't know what to say. Lacey's leaving hurt bad.

Maggie wrapped her arm around me. "I know it's tough right now, Tom, but there'll be another girl. You're quite a catch." She winked. "How about breakfast?"

"Sure, Maggie," I said, and suddenly realized that with Maggie here I didn't have to run the cafe anymore. It came back to me how scared I'd been when I first heard I had to do it and how miserable that day turned out to be—until Lacey showed up. I took a long look toward the Coloma Road, hoping for a last glimpse of Lacey. Right now I'd gladly give all the gold in California if only I could just spend one more day in the cafe with her.

"Goodbye, Lacey," I whispered. "I love you."

Bonus Read
THE YUBA TROUBLE
Racism and romance in the California gold rush
Coming soon

A long day of hard riding across the rocky ground beside the stream had drained me. A hot meal and a night's sleep would be welcome. A raft of small birds sang happily from the forest, their constant chatter fluttering over the roar of the gushing South Yuba River as it frothed along, overwhelmed with snowmelt from the mountains.

I headed west on the north bank. The first faint shouts came just after I'd passed three men mining a small bar. The screams set in soon after. Ungodly shrieks that went on and on. A shot rang out. More shouts. More shrieks—louder—longer. Another shot.

Then silence.

An eerie, spine-chilling silence.

The rumble of the river thundered unbroken in my ears, the chirp of birds gone. I'd come upstream this afternoon. Directly downstream no one camped save those with me, those who now waited for my return. A cold shiver thundered down my back. Sweat flushed from my forehead.

Like a fire built from damp wood realization smoldered slow before the blaze of truth flashed bright across my mind. I nudged my horse faster. I let him run. He knew the way. A dread welled from deep inside me. It couldn't be. It wasn't possible.

The river bent to the northwest. I rode on. Smoke filled my nostrils, the sweet smell of meat cooking, the bitter stench of burning flesh. The camp was close. I reined my horse to a walk and yanked the shotgun from its scabbard.

Here huge pines grew close to the river. A creek flowed into the Yuba from the northeast. The camp sat in a clearing on the far side, past a line of scrub oak. Nothing moved, no sound came save the rushing water, the birds quiet, hiding, afraid.

And so was I.

But I had to know. Two friends were in that camp. Where

they okay?

I urged my horse on. He stepped into the open, charged across the stream, bulled past the brush and into the clearing.

And then I screamed.

The body hung above the fire, dangling by a rope tied around his wrists and looped across a limb. Naked but for a sack over his head, slowly twisting to and fro, feet well-nigh burned away. High on his left arm a bullet wound, a second one in the heart. The killer, at least, showed some shred of mercy.

I had to get him down, away from a fire set only with the unholy end of roasting a man alive. I leaped from my horse, kicked the unburned wood clear then stomped embers and coals until they were black dust, threw a blanket down over the ashes and cut the rope. He tumbled into a heap. I drug him away and covered his shame.

One dead, another missing, they had no money, no enemies. It made no sense. I swore a solemn oath to find the killer, make him pay, an eye for an eye as it should be. And there my recollections overran me, sweeping me back to where it all began . . .

Thanks for reading

INTO THE FACE OF THE DEVIL

If you enjoyed the book, please leave a short review on the book page at Amazon.com. Reviews are helpful to other readers as well as to both Amazon and the author.

CPSIA information can be obtained
at www.ICGtesting.com
Printed in the USA
FSOW03n2304060617
35073FS